Martha Jordan Craig

The Setting Son

24 23 22 21 20 19   8 7 6 5 4 3 2 1

THE SETTING SON

Published by:
Emerge Publishing, LLC
9521B Riverside Parkway, Suite 243
Tulsa, Oklahoma 74137
Phone: 888.407.4447
www.EmergePublishing.com

Library of Congress Cataloging-in-Publication Data

ISBN: 978-1-949758-07-8 Paperback
ISBN: 978-1-949758-08-5 Digital/E-book
Audiobook available at www.Audible.com or www.Amazon.com

BISAC Category:
FIC066000 FICTION / Small Town & Rural
FIC074000 FICTION / Southern

Printed in the United States

I hope you love
Mookie Frye!
Martha Jordan
Oct. 2019

The Setting Son

MARTHA JORDAN CRAIG

emerge
publishing

TULSA, OKLAHOMA

Table of Contents

Dedication

I dedicate this book to Oklahoma Bull Rider, Roy Dell Barnes and all of the other athletes that give everything they have to the sport they love.

Roy Dell Barnes, riding on the back of #117, was paralyzed by a career-ending bull riding accident. He loved bull riding and the thrill that came with trying his best to hang on for the entire eight seconds.

The name of the bull…Untouchable. I salute you, Roy Dell.

Acknowledgments

First and foremost, I would like to thank my best friend, who happens to be my husband, Rick Craig, for being my helpful and most loving cheerleader. Thank you, honey, for the hours you spent allowing me to read every single word of the manuscript to you…more than once. You are the best!

Next, I would like to thank two of my very best friends, Jack and Terrie Wimer, for gifting me the use of their lake cottage, nestled within their breathtaking Abiquiu, perched on the shores of Grand Lake O' The Cherokees in Grove, Oklahoma. What an inspiration! I will never forget the hospitality or the pelicans!

To my son and daughter-in-law, Chris and Meghan Jenkins, mere words cannot express how wonderful it was to have the opportunity to sit and write many chapters of this book in your gorgeous Evergreen, Colorado home in the majestic Rocky Mountains. It was truly an inspiration. Thanks so very much.

Alice O'Malley and her clan at KGiL Farm in Nowata, Oklahoma, beckoned me to come to their piece of heaven in Green Country and find writing inspiration around all things cows and cow patties. I'm glad I took them up on their offer. Where else to be inspired to write about Oklahoma rodeos?

I can't thank my two dear friends, Eldon and Carolyn Mercer, enough for letting this gypsy writer find comfort and inspiration in their loving and beautiful home in Miami, Oklahoma. I'll be forever grateful to you both.

Big thanks go to my precious and long-time friend, Marilyn (Unger) Maple for granting her permission to add her story to this book. I'm still in awe, Cowgirl!

I couldn't have had a better source for my riveting research question, "Who brought the biggest and baddest bulls to Oklahoma rodeos in the 1970's?" Mighty thanks to you, Roy Dell Barnes, for all your help and for allowing me to make you a character in this book. You are one great cowboy!

Lastly, I offer up many heartfelt thanks to my publishing partners, Christian Ophus, Julie Werner, and the entire team at Emerge Publishing. You have provided the most comprehensive range of publishing services and options available and I am grateful for this partnership. I look forward to experiencing together what lies ahead.

CHAPTER 1:

Soggy Cap'n Crunch

Every weekday morning for as long as he could remember, Mookie Frye concentrated on the ratio of milk to cereal down to the very last bite. He hated soggy Cap'n Crunch cereal. If there was more milk than cereal, he would shake the box carefully until the perfect balance of milk to cereal was met. A good morning was when Mookie was able to lift his bowl up to his mouth to drizzle the last bit of milk onto his tongue, satisfied that every bite of cereal had been crispy, yet covered with the cold milk.

This morning was different. Mookie had let his Cap'n Crunch cereal get very soggy. He sat alone at the small kitchen table gazing out the window with his chin in his hand. He knew that he needed to leave for school in ten minutes. The small cuckoo clock hanging on the wall ticked off each second with its familiar rhythmic sound. Besides the clinking of his spoon in his cereal bowl, the consistent ticking was the only other sound in the entire house. As if being propelled by its own force, Mookie's right hand pushed the spoon around the bowl swirling mushy bits of yellow cereal into a whirlpool of lukewarm milk. This was not a good morning.

She thought he didn't see her black eye.

Mookie's mother, Hannah Frye, had spent the early morning hours gently patting her CoverGirl concealer onto her upper right cheekbone and sweeping it ever so carefully around the outside of her right eye. The pain was getting worse by the minute. The trickle of blood had stopped around midnight when she finally crawled into bed. Up by 4:30 am, Hannah looked at her reflection in the bathroom mirror and saw that her cheek had swollen twice its normal size, and the bluish tint of a bruise was beginning to discolor her pretty right eye. She knew quite well that she couldn't let her son Mookie see her like this.

By 6:30 am, Hannah realized that she had done all she could do to try and disguise her injuries as she pushed her makeup drawer shut. With one last sideways glance in the mirror, she headed toward the kitchen to prepare Mookie's breakfast. Down the hallway behind her son's bedroom door, she heard the sound of Mookie's radio alarm. Hannah recognized the voice of the sportscaster, Denny Matthews, as he was giving the recap for last night's Kansas City Royals baseball game.

Hannah caught herself before she fell in a heap in the kitchen doorway, tears streaming down her face. Stick loved the Kansas City Royals.

She missed Stick so badly.

CHAPTER 2:

Milton Edward Frye

Hannah Kimball met Milton Frye in Tishomingo, Oklahoma in the summer of 1971. Milton was known by the rodeo community by his well-deserved nickname of Stick-Tight (after the scratchy and obnoxious bur). The nickname came about by his almost supernatural ability to stay for the full eight seconds or more atop any freight train, disguised as a bull, that he found his rear end straddling.

Stick was somewhat of a legend in the southern parts of Oklahoma. He had been riding bulls like a tick on the back of a hound since he was twelve years old. His dad, Ed "Boots" Frye, had been a pretty salty bull rider in his day, so it was a given that he would sooner, rather than later, pass the torch to his young son. There had never been anyone like Stick Frye.

When Stick was seven, his dad, Boots, fashioned him his own bull riding apparatus out of an old cutup tire, two long ropes, two old rusted springs, and a sturdy piece of latigo leather. Boots tied the ropes between two pin oak trees in the backyard and, at the midway point, made a bull's body from the cut-up tire. He attached the springs in between the rope and the bull. The latigo leather was wrapped around and positioned where Stick could grab hold of it with one hand and throw the other hand up in the air. Just like the pros. Boots had found an old ticking covered mattress in the barn and placed it in their "arena", under the bull, in case the boy flew off into the air.

The father and son duo decided that when Stick was ready to go, he would turn to his dad and nod. Boots Frye never had more fun in his life than when he would try his darnedest to shake his seven-year-old son off that "bull". He would bounce him up and down and all around. The boy never budged an inch. He held on for dear life.

"Hang on a minute, son, I'm going to go get your mother. She's got to see this!" Boots Frye said to Stick while laughing so hard that he had tears running down his face.

"Marlene! Marlene! Come here. You've just got to see what we're doin' out here."

Marlene Frye dusted off her flour covered hands and started hurrying out to the backyard, wiping her hands on her apron as she went.

Just as she stepped off the porch out into the yard, she saw her young son go bouncing up and down in the air. He was all hunkered over with his knees squeezing tight to the bull. Mashed down on his head was one of Boots' old straw, cowboy hats. Little Stick was smiling like a Cheshire cat, with one arm up in the air and hollering "Yee Haw!"

"Edward Frye! What are you doing to my baby? He's going to break his neck if he falls off!"

Marlene Frye was outnumbered as she stood and watched, shaking her head as her husband shook the tar out of her only child on that bucking bull, time after time. He never fell off. Just like a stick-tight bur.

After school and the chores were done, Stick and Boots spent many evenings in their makeshift arena. Boots, trying to think of new ways to sling the ropes, with Stick holding on like a clamp.

They eventually wore the old bull out. They had named him "Tooty Frooty" and both felt sad the day ol' Tooty, made from the used tire, split, and frayed for the last time.

Even so, it wasn't long before a neighbor down the road allowed them to train with a couple of his feisty young bulls, and before too long Boots had Stick straddled on the bulls' backs and the neighborhood rodeo was in full swing.

Boots and Marlene Frye loaded up their pickup truck every Friday afternoon, as almost every weekend of Stick's childhood, they had him entered in all the junior rodeos in the state.

It was pretty much a given that Stick Frye would sweep every prize category offered up with his natural, God-given ability, to plant his rear on a bull and hang solid until the clock ran out.

Stick loved the rodeo. It was in his blood. Winning felt good, and he made his parents proud.

However, unlike his father, Stick Frye had another passion that filled him with joy as much as bull riding. Baseball.

CHAPTER 3:

Stick's Choice

As he became a young man, Stick Frye knew he needed to make a choice between his two loves, rodeo or baseball. He excelled at both.

The summer after his senior year at Tishomingo High School, there was a never-ending line of baseball scouts sitting in the bleachers as Stick Frye rocked and fired pitch after pitch, strike after strike, to almost every opponent on the local American Legion summer league teams. The offers were coming in from almost every big-league farm club and college in the nation. The letters and phone calls beckoned him to choose their program, with hopes to get in the big leagues or to pick a school program and get a college degree to boot.

Simultaneously, he was continuing to dominate the high school bull riding circuit in Oklahoma. The promise of a career in the rodeo with big payoffs was very enticing and Stick knew he would have to make his decision very soon.

One hot afternoon, as he was taking some pre-game practice pitches, Stick Frye lost his concentration when he happened to glance over toward the bleachers and noticed someone sitting in the sun. She was the prettiest girl he had ever seen.

The Tishomingo American Legion team was playing a team from nearby Madill, Oklahoma. She was sitting on the visitor's side.

"She must have a boyfriend on the Madill team," Stick said just above a whisper as he sat down in the dugout after the bottom of the eighth inning.

"Who are you talking about, Stick? She who?" Stick's teammate Bobby Kimball said as he threw his ball glove on the bench and placed his foot up to tie his shoe.

Stick didn't realize he had said it that loud, but he figured he might as well fess up.

"That blonde over there in the yellow sun dress, walking over to the line for snow cones."

"Oh her! That's my cousin Hannah. She lives in Madill. Since Madill is playing our team they came over to see me play and…"

Stick interrupted Bobby before he could finish his sentence.

"Her boyfriend?" Stick said as he looked down at a bug crawling under the bench.

"Nah, I don't think she has one. She came to see me and her brother Jack play."

CHAPTER 4

Stick Falls for Hannah

As soon as Tishomingo put the hurts on the baseball team from Madill, Stick Frye crammed his bat and ball glove into his duffle bag, hoisted it up on his shoulder and made a beeline for the Madill side of the stadium. He didn't waste a minute before he was standing conspicuously behind Bobby's cousin, Hannah.

With his baseball cap cocked on the back of his head, sweaty trails of dirt streaming down the sides of his face, Stick was mouthing the words "introduce me to her" to his friend who was standing directly in front of his cousin, Hannah.

"Oh, yeah, hey, Hannah, turn around here. I want to introduce you to my friend, Stick."

Hannah twirled around and saw a tall, good looking young man with a captivating smile stamped on his face.

"Hi, Stick. I'm Hannah. From Madill. Remember Madill? The team you guys just clobbered unmercifully out there on the field." She was grinning, and he was blushing.

"Yeah, too bad there's no run rule on this league. We would have had you out of this hot sun a whole lot sooner." He shot back playfully.

She was feisty. It was love at first banter.

CHAPTER 5:

Muskogee Bound

Stick Frye had made up his mind to have his decision made between baseball and the rodeo after the coming weekend. At the last rodeo, Stick's dad had seen a poster tacked up on the billboard. He recognized the event right away. It was the annual bull riding showdown in Muskogee, Oklahoma. The Okie 100 with Barnes and Sons Bucking Stock. Guaranteed to be the meanest, toughest batch of bulls anywhere around.

Boots knew his son Stick was ready for this competition. It would be his first full on battle to the finish with the big boys. Boots' eyes lit up as he continued to read the poster. In large letters he saw that the guest announcer would be none other than Jim Shoulders, the "Babe Ruth" of rodeo. Jim had won five PRCA world championships in the 1950's. Boots couldn't wait to tell his son. Stick would be so excited to hear that he would have the chance to meet his idol face to face.

Stick was psyched, and Boots mailed in the entry fee.

The Frye family had relatives in Broken Arrow, Oklahoma. Marlene's first cousin, Harriet Looper, had invited them to stay with her and her family for the short daily trip over to Muskogee for the rodeo.

It had been raining for three days straight. Early Thursday morning, Boots loaded up his family and headed to Broken Arrow from their home in Tishomingo. Just before he pulled out of their driveway, Boots thumbed through the pages of the Farmer's Almanac he had placed in his lap and saw that the sun should be popping out right about the time they were to arrive. It was mostly thunder and lightning in their area but word from Harriett was a steady rainfall had not let up in northeast Oklahoma since Tuesday.

CHAPTER 6:

The Fryes Bunk with the Loopers

Boots Frye made record time as he commandeered his Ford F250 crew cab truck from Tishomingo to Broken Arrow on that cloudy summer morning in Oklahoma. The Farmer's Almanac's prediction of sunshine on the horizon came true as Marlene and Boots reached for their visors at the same time. Marlene's shaded the passenger side of the truck perfectly, but Boots had to squint as he made a couple of sharp turns. The glare was the brightest smack dab between the two visors and it made it a bit difficult for Boots to keep the truck on his side of the road.

"Hey, Dad, isn't that Aunt Harriet and Uncle Bud's house up there on the left?" Stick had been staring out the window the entire trip to Broken Arrow, and Boots was relieved to hear his son's voice from the back seat. Boots had been wondering if his teenage son was nervous about his first adult rodeo. He had a room full of saddles, trophies and buckles back at their house from junior rodeos all over the creation, but he had never

13

been this quiet on a trip to any of those events. Stick Frye was a household name in the junior rodeo circuit. Boots even came to the conclusion that his son, Stick, to be downright honest, was pretty darn famous. It was unheard of for a kid in the junior rodeos to have a sponsor. Stick Frye, the kid from Tishomingo, Oklahoma, had one. He was sponsored by his grandparents' grocery store back in Tishomingo. "Grandparents or not, he has a sponsor." Boots Frye smiled to himself as he thought about that. Boots was so proud of Stick and extremely confident that his son could hold his own in the arena. He had a natural ability - just like his old man.

"Why, it sure is, son. Thank God. I was getting tired of driving blind." Boots joked as he made a funny face at his son in the rearview mirror. Stick half grinned at his dad. Boots thought Stick looked almost green. "Maybe he is just car sick." Boots thought to himself.

Aunt Harriet came bursting out of her screen door and was halfway down the driveway before Boots had the truck put in park. She was tip toeing and jumping over mud puddles as she ran, hopped, splashed, and hollered, happy to see her kinfolks as they arrived at her home. Uncle Bud was waving at their guests as he flew past them on a riding lawn mower. He was wearing madras plaid shorts, an unbuttoned long sleeved, striped, pearl button cowboy shirt, and unlaced chukka boots. His mutton chop side burns and hair down to his collar were blowing backwards in the wind. Wet grass and mud were spewing out the back of the mower as Uncle Bud splashed through a big puddle in the yard. "I'll be right back, I have to hose this mower off. I tried, but I guess I won't be doin' much mowin' today." Uncle Bud yelled as he disappeared around the side of the house.

"Howdy folks, howdy! Come here and let me hug your necks." Aunt Harriet squealed as she threw her arms up in the air and waited for the first Frye to be encircled in her embrace.

It was safe to say that Uncle Bud and Aunt Harriet were Stick Frye's most favorite relatives in the whole wide world. They were generous, thoughtful, loving, kind, and most of all, flat-out hilarious. Stick was running toward his Aunt Harriet with his arms raised as high as hers. "Sticktight, you sweet doodlebug, when did you get so dang tall?" Stick grabbed his aunt, picked her up and whirled her around and around, plopping her right back where he had scooped her up. She was petite and spunky. "Angie! Trey! Marlene, Boots, and Stick are here!" Aunt Harriet hollered toward the house as her nephew sat her back down. Trey came bounding out of the house with a mile-wide grin on his face. Trey and Stick were the same age, give or take a few pushes. Born on the same day, about one minute apart.

"Where is Angie?" Harriet asked Trey.

"I tried to let her know but she had her record player up too loud, Mom. All I could hear was her screeching to Temptation Eyes by the Grassroots." Trey said as he shook his head and rolled his eyes.

"Let's go scare her, Trey." Stick started toward the house as he grabbed his cousin Trey by arm.

Aunt Harriet walked between Marlene and Boots with her arms around their waists as they headed toward the front door of her house. She showed them to their room and instructed them to get settled in, as she almost had supper ready.

Meanwhile, Trey and Stick had concocted a plan to scare the bejeezus out of Angie. It was their lucky day as they sneaked around the back of the house, squatted down behind the garden shed, and saw that Angie had her bedroom window wide open. She was enjoying the summer afternoon breeze with her record player cranked up as loud as it would go. It was all they could do to not bust a gut laughing as they saw her standing on her bed, with her hairbrush-microphone in her hand, eyes closed, belting out her best singalong to Temptation Eyes.

"ohhhhh, temptation eyes, looking through my,my,my soul...."

Trey had pulled a garden hose out of the shed and stuck the end of it up to Angie's window screen. His job was to hold it steady and Stick's was to go around the side of the house and start wailing a ghost moan into the other end of the hose, overpowering the beat of the Grassroots' song bouncing off Angie's walls.

"well, temptation eyes, you've gotta love me, gotta love me, tonight"

She didn't notice it for a bit, but when she did, they almost lost it. She stopped mid "gotta love me, baby, yeah, mmmmm" and jumped off her bed. Angie Looper stood motionless with her eyes as big as silver dollars.

Stick had recently attended a marathon movie extravaganza at the Indie Theatre in Tishomingo. For $1.00, a person could watch the 1959 thriller, The House on Haunted Hill, starring Vincent Price, three times in a row. By the end of the third viewing, Stick Frye could do a ghost moan that would have made Watson Pritchard's dead brother proud.

"Oooooh-ohhhhhh. Oooooh-ohhhhhh...."

Angie crept over to her small record player and lifted the arm, so the needle wouldn't touch the record.

"Ooooooooooohhhhhhhhh. Oooooooooohhhhh..."

Her voice was barely above a whisper. "Who is there? Mom? Dad? Trey?"

Stick gave it his best bellow and moan, and Angie bolted toward her bedroom door, screaming like a banshee as she ran.

Stick and Trey were rolling on the grass in the backyard, laughing so hard that they couldn't breathe. As she ran down the hall, Angie glanced toward the patio door and saw her brother and cousin with their hands on their stomachs, laughing their heads off.

"Those two are such spazzes!" she shrieked. Not to be outdone, Angie immediately ran out through the front door, around to the side of the house where Stick had dropped his end of the hose, and quickly hooked it to the faucet, cranking the handle to turn the water on at full blast.

Unfortunately for the two spazzes, Trey still had his end of the hose in his hand.

The battle was on. Angie was watching and laughing from inside the house. She had her thumbs in her ears, waving her fingers at the boys and giving them the raspberries. Trey and Stick, both soaking wet, yelled at her to come on out if she thought she was so tough.

She did, and they had a blast spraying each other with the hose.

Stick, Trey, and Angie had many years of memories growing up together. Cousins they were. But to Stick, they were the siblings he never had.

"And Lord, please bless us and bless this food. Oh and, Lord, we want to ask you to please excuse our kids, Trey, Angie, and Stick, for acting like kindergarteners instead of high schoolers. Amen." Uncle Bud ended his prayer with a wink and a grin. Everyone laughed a hearty laugh as Aunt Harriet passed the heaping platter of fried chicken around the table.

After the last spoonful of peach cobbler was licked clean, Boots asked if anyone wanted to take a drive over to Muskogee, to walk around and look at the rodeo arena. The opening ceremonies would be tomorrow at 6:00 pm and Boots thought it might be a good idea to let Stick get the feel of the arena before his first ride. It was 100% yes, and they all piled into Uncle Bud's hippie VW van for the forty-five-minute trip.

There was a bustle of activity going on at the fairgrounds when Uncle Bud pulled the van into a parking spot. Stick was the last one to get out, and Boots looked over at his son as Stick peered at the entryway to the arena. Boots couldn't get a feel for what was going through Stick's mind as he was unusually quiet on the way to Muskogee.

"Son, you doin' alright?" Boots spun around and spoke to Stick as they walked toward the arena. The three kids were bringing up the rear.

"Stick? Son? You okay?" Stick's face had a blank stare planted all over it.

"What, Dad? What did you say?" Stick almost ran into his dad when Boots stopped in front of him.

"I said are you okay? You're walking around like a robot."

Stick chuckled. "I guess I am, huh? I suppose I was remembering coming here last summer and it looks like everything grew a lot bigger since then. I know that's the same entryway we walked through to get in there, but somehow it looks like they came here and replaced everything with all giant-sized stuff!" Everyone laughed, and Aunt Harriet walked over and patted her nephew on the back.

"It'll be okay, Stick. I think we better pray that the bulls they bring in here aren't giant-sized." Aunt Harriet quipped as she offered him a piece of Juicy Fruit gum from her purse.

Stick Frye couldn't have agreed with his Aunt Harriet more and was getting ready to say something else until the sound of an oncoming tractor interrupted their conversation.

Boots watched as three tractors, pulling large rakes and drags, drove past them. Following the tractors were two dump trucks loaded with topsoil.

Prepping an arena for a rodeo was part of the process but something about the amount of dirt being brought in had Boots Frye curious.

"Hey, Bud, why do you think they are hauling in so much dirt?"

Uncle Bud, adjusted his red ballcap emblazoned with a big white dove and the words "Woodstock, 3 Days of Peace & Music" (he didn't attend the rock and folk festival, but his brother Dwayne did and brought back the cap as a souvenir).

"Well, Boots, I guess it's because of the gully washer last night. It rained really hard for about three hours. They must have had to fill in some mighty big mud holes."

Boots continued to watch the action on the field of the arena as the tractors drove around, raking the dirt clods to powder as they went.

Maybe Boots had eaten too fast or too much because he was starting to get heartburn. The more he stood watching the grounds crew, the more the acid formed in his throat.

"Marlene, do you have any Tums in your purse?" Boots whispered to his wife. She immediately started to dig around in her denim handbag, pulling out the tin of anti-acid tablets. Marlene handed over two to her husband and he tossed them into his mouth, chewing and swallowing the cakey tablets and hoping for a speedy relief.

The mission of letting Stick wander around the arena had been circumvented by the grounds crew. Boots decided they were probably in the way of the workers and the unanimous decision to leave had them piling back in the van and heading home to Broken Arrow, to get a good night's sleep. At least that was the plan.

As great plans sometimes go awry, Boots Frye never shut his eyes after his head hit the pillow. Down the hall in the top bunk in his cousin Trey's room, Stick Frye tossed and turned until the neighborhood rooster crowed an obnoxious cock-a-doodle-doo.

It was Friday. Stick would be planted on the back of a bull named Big Brutus in a little over twelve hours. The countdown had begun.

CHAPTER 7

The Okie 100 and the Legends of Yore

The opening ceremony was action packed and patriotic. The great Jim Shoulders welcomed the crowd by first introducing the local chapter of the Muskogee Boy Scouts as twelve young troop members walked out on the bandstand, flags held high, as they presented the colors.

"Welcome, folks, to the Okie 100! Thelbert Barnes has assured me that he has brought some monster bulls to the beautiful city of Muskogee, Oklahoma! Are we ready to witness a train wreck or two?" The crowd went bonkers. "Who in this crowd is ready to say the Pledge of Allegiance to the greatest country on earth?" Jim Shoulders had the crowd up on their feet, clapping and whooping and hollering.

"Looks like we all are! Well, first off, I would like y'all to look over at the bandstand. Walkin' up those steps is a pretty little lady by the name of JoJo Riley. Miss Riley is gonna start this opening ceremony off with our national anthem. Gentlemen, please remove your hats and let's all place our hands on our hearts."

Fourteen-year-old JoJo Riley belted out the national anthem and was given a thunderous applause.

"How many of you are ready for a good time on a Friday night?" More applause came from the crowd as Jim Shoulders got them all revved up. "That's what I like to hear 'cause we're ready to have a good time on this Friday night. It's about to get wild and crazy around here, folks. This is the day we've been waitin' for. Barnes and Sons showed up with the meanest and toughest bunch of buckin' stock this side of the old Mississippi!" Jim Shoulders spoke directly into the face of the silver microphone as he stood up and leaned out of the announcer's box. The crowd went wild.

"I'm tellin' ya those bulls have been back there eatin' nails, so they won't be shy. No, they won't be shy." The crowd laughed a hearty laugh as he continued.

"So, let's get this party started! Give a mighty hand clap to the Muskogee Junior Round Up Club as they bust out here in the arena."

The first four cowgirls on their sleek horses came charging through the gate to deafening applause from the enthusiastic crowd. There was a band, primed and ready on the bandstand, that struck up a robust rendition of "Big Balls in Cowtown" as the pennants were set, and the next group of performers galloped into the arena. Each of the eight riders on horseback carried a large American flag while they raced around the arena sashaying in and out and circling each other in the grand march as the red, white, and blue of the flags waved and flapped in the wind.

It was show-time and Stick Frye was nervous. It wasn't a lack of confidence that was making him tense and edgy, but he just couldn't put his finger on why he had a heaviness that he had never quite experienced before in his eighteen years. He had been hanging out with all the other bull riders over by the bull pens. Their names and faces were all legendary in the rodeo world of the tri-state area. Oklahoma, Missouri, and Kansas, all boasted that they each offered up the toughest cowboys. The bulls were humongous, and it didn't take Stick long to find out that he was the youngest contestant entered in the bull riding event.

The other bull riders had been very nice to him. Teasing him a little, but generally letting him know they had all been where he was at that moment in time. Stick was awestruck, and tongue-tied, hanging out with the group of seasoned cowboys that he had been idolizing his whole born days, so when they offered unsolicited advice, he hung onto their every word.

The bull rider entered in the Muskogee rodeo that came with astronomical credentials in the area of winning at bull riding, was none other than Roy Dell Barnes from Tahlequah, Oklahoma. The Oklahoma daredevil wearing chaps, boots and a Stetson hat with a prominent Montana crease, would bring the crowds to their feet every single time he mounted a brawny and burly bovine. He was known for his tenacity and insatiable desire to put the biggest buttload of points on the leaderboard. Roy Dell Barnes was determined to be as high in the standings as possible - a feat he achieved more often than not. He was definitely a legend in his own time.

It was a muggy night in Muskogee, Oklahoma. The rain was gone but it left the air filled with sweltering and sticky humidity. Cowboys took their hats off and wiped their brows on their shirtsleeves, women fanned themselves and their infants with the event programs, and the kids ran around getting sweaty, muddy, and having the times of their lives. It was the rodeo.

Stick had decided to head over to find his family in the stands and catch the rest of the grand opening ceremonies. As he started to climb down from his perch on the fence around the bull pens, he felt two soft hands cover his eyes. "Guess who?"

It was Hannah.

Following a whirlwind courtship, Stick had gotten down on one knee a month prior and asked the cutest girl in Oklahoma to be his sidekick for the rest of his life. After a lot of tears and sweet kisses she bubbled out a "yes, of course I will, Stick" and the wedding plans got off to a great start. Hannah had told Stick that she really wanted to be in Muskogee to see him ride, but her Sunday School class was giving her a bridal shower the same weekend. Stick told her he understood, but deep down inside he wanted Hannah to be in the stands this weekend, in Muskogee, Oklahoma. He wanted it in the worst way. In fact, it came very close to bothering him. He needed her to be at this rodeo and he couldn't figure out why it was eating away at him so badly. When Stick turned around and saw her standing in front of him, he knew instantly that it had been a little white lie, so she could surprise him and cheer loudly from the stands for her cowboy. He almost went white with relief.

Hannah's dad had gotten his family a motel room in Muskogee for the weekend, so he and his wife could accompany their daughter to this all-important rodeo. As the Kimballs led the way to the bleachers, Stick and Hannah walked hand in hand to sit with Boots and Marlene in the stands. Hannah chattered on and on how they wouldn't have missed this rodeo for anything in the world. Stick only heard parts of the conversation as he was focused on how nice Hannah's hand felt in his hand, and how beautiful she looked in her hip hugger jeans and white peasant blouse. He felt all warm inside thinking about how her tanned skin and blonde hair sparkled in the lights surrounding the rodeo arena. He loved Hannah

Kimball with everything in him. He loved her with a deep, and abiding love and couldn't stop thinking about his desire to take her as his bride and love and protect her for the rest of his life.

Stick had no clue why he was feeling so sappy, and worried. Maybe it was how his future, and now hers, was hinging on the outcome of this rodeo. If he made a decent showing on the scoreboard, he knew he had a very big decision to make. Rodeo or baseball. The choice was huge but no matter which way he went, Stick Frye was satisfied knowing that Hannah was going with him. She was his sidekick for life.

"Yoo hoo! Here we are!" Marlene Frye stood up and waved the embroidered hankie she held in her hand. She had her hair up in a French twist and when little trickles of sweat would run down the back of her neck, she would wipe them away with the hankie. Boots and Marlene had gotten there early enough to snag really good seats in the stands. Stick and the others waved back and headed up the stairs to join the Fryes, Aunt Harriet, Uncle Bud, Trey and Angie.

Bull riding would be the last and most anticipated event of the evening. Stick was able to watch all the barrel racing, bull dogging and the first three contestants on the bucking broncs before he left the stands to go prepare for his ride on the back of Big Brutus. He gave Hannah a quick peck on her cheek and she, in turn, gave him a big hug, and off he went back to the bucking chutes.

Of the eight riders that went before him, only three had been able to put a score on the board. Thelbert Barnes' bucking stock had certainly lived up to their claim to fame. The bulls that were pawing and snorting in the corrals looked possessed by demons. The instant the bull riders found their spots on the devils' backs, shook their heads to signal that they were ready, it was a flurry of flying bull riders that landed flat on their faces, backs, and butts, before they realized they had even shot out of the gate.

When Friday night came to a close, Roy Dell Barnes was in the lead. Stick was pretty darn satisfied with his ride on the back of Big Brutus and couldn't complain that his first time in the big leagues had him going into Saturday night's finals holding onto fourth place. He had gone the full eight seconds, which was in his mind a miracle, and accepted his score that had seen several deductions for lack of control and his not-so-fluid movements. Big Brutus scored high for his athleticism and how difficult he made it for Stick to stay on board. "Staying alive was far and above more important than style." Stick mumbled to himself as he looked up to see his score. He was dusting his chaps off with his hand when he looked over and saw his dad.

Boots Frye had wanted to get a closer look when his son rode Big Brutus, so he scurried down the stadium steps and joined the other cowboys up on the fence with a bird's eye view from the bucking chute area. When Stick finished his ride, and came out of the arena, his proud dad grabbed him in a big bear hug. "Fantastic ride, son! I couldn't be prouder and tomorrow night will be one for the record books. I just know it!"

CHAPTER 8:

The Great Trepidation

To celebrate Stick's feat of being on the leaderboard, they decided to hurry over to Slick's Bar B Que in a small building on 24th and Shawnee in downtown Muskogee. Alonzo "Slick" Smith had been serving up his famous smoked meats, slathered with his secret sauce, since around 1950. They ate and ate until they thought they would explode.

Stick walked Hannah to her parents' car, gave her a sweet kiss, hugged her mom, and shook her dad's hand.

"See y'all tomorrow!" Hannah said to the Fryes, as she smiled, waved, and got into the back seat of her parents' baby blue Nash Rambler.

Back at the Looper's home in Broken Arrow, it took Stick Frye a long time to settle down enough in his head to finally get to sleep. The uneasy feeling just wouldn't go away. However, it was lights out for his cousin, Trey, as he fell fast asleep in the lower bunk as soon as his head hit the pillow. Not so much for Stick, as he tossed and turned for hours before exhaustion finally overcame his restlessness.

Down the hallway, in the guest bedroom, Boots was also having difficulty falling asleep. The barbeque was delicious, but he had eaten way too much. Thank goodness Marlene still had her tin of Tums. Boots popped a couple of tablets into his mouth and finally drifted off to sleep.

Heartburn has a strange way of causing weird, alarming, and scary dreams. Boots sat straight up in bed. He wasn't quite awake and couldn't figure out where he was. As he got his bearings, he heard himself softly whimpering and taking short, choppy breaths.

"Honey! Boots, are you okay? What's wrong?" Marlene sat up on her side of the bed, sprang to her feet, and was standing by Boots' side of the bed in a flash.

"Oh, man, what a horrible nightmare. That scared the liver out of me." Boots had his hand on his chest and was looking up at Marlene like he had just seen a ghost.

"What in the world did you dream? What was it?" Marlene sat down on the bed by Boots, placing her hand on his shoulder.

When Boots Frye realized what he had just dreamed, he knew that he could never tell Marlene. Never. He was sweating profusely and if the light was turned on, he was convinced that Marlene would tell him that he was as white as Casper the Friendly Ghost.

There was no way he could tell Marlene the truth.

"Oh, nothin', Marlene. It was stupid. Just a heartburn-induced crazy nightmare. I've got to quit eating so much stinkin' food so close to bed time. Now, get back in bed. I'm sorry I woke you up."

Boots Frye didn't close his eye the rest of the night. He couldn't shake what he had seen in his dream. It was horrible. He could never tell Marlene.

El Diablo

The ambulance arrived about two minutes after Boots Frye scaled the fence and made it to Stick in the middle of the arena. As he ran as hard as he could toward his only child, Boots started loosening the bandana that was tied around his neck.

"Don't move him! Don't lift the bull off him yet!" Boots yelled at the gathering crowd as he was already down on his side, frantically pushing one end of the bandana underneath his son's arm as he made it into a tourniquet. "I need a couple more!" By that time, a crowd of cowboys encircled the area where Stick lay motionless, underneath the bull. The bull was named El Diablo.

Instantly, multi-colored bandanas appeared near his face as Boots grabbed the closest two and secured them tightly around his son's arm, right next to the area where the bull's horn was lodged deep inside Stick's bicep. Smack dab in an artery.

CHAPTER 9: EL DIABLO

Stick was spread eagle on his back, and the gargantuan bull was flipped over on its side, directly on top of Stick, with his right horn smashed deep into the flesh of Stick's arm. Blood was gushing. El Diablo's right, back leg was broken and twisted from sinking into the mud hole. Stick lay unconscious, barely able to breathe from the weight of the bull pressing hard on his chest. Boots Frye was in full-on "dad mode".

"I'm here, son. If you can hear me, squeeze my hand." Nothing. Nothing but shallow breathing as Boots spoke into Stick's ear. "We're gonna get this guy off you right now. I won't leave you, buddy. I won't ever leave you. Hang on, son. Please just hang on."

"Okay, we're ready! Lift him up!" Boots yelled at the group of twenty men that were positioned to lift the bull off Stick.

"On the count of three, boys!" someone hollered out. "One, two and three!"

The bull pawed and fought but the adrenaline spiked cowboys had no trouble getting El Diablo lifted off Stick Frye's chest.

Boots gasped as he looked down at his son, lying in a huge pool of blood.

"Oh, dear God. What have I done?" Boots Frye sank back down to his knees beside Stick's mangled body and covered his face with his hands.

"Let's check for a pulse," the paramedic barked at his co-worker as he knelt beside Stick and Boots.

"Get out of the way, sir."

"I ain't leavin'. Work around me. I ain't leavin' my boy."

The entire audience was on their feet with their mouths gaping open. Someone in the crowd said, "Oh, dear God."

30

CHAPTER 10:

Boots Frye and the Foreboding

After Stick was loaded into the ambulance with his dad crouching down right beside the gurney, the paramedic slammed the door and started around the side of the vehicle to take the driver's seat.

"Which hospital you takin' him? We're family." It was Uncle Bud. He had followed close behind Boots down the stairs to the arena and had been one of the twenty men to lift El Diablo off Stick.

"Mercy General. Tulsa. You in that van over there?"

"Yes, that's the boy's mother and the rest of the family. We'll follow you."

Roy Dell Barnes had secured the lead very early on that Saturday night and it was a fight to the finish for second place. Danny Douthitt was dusting his hat off on the side of his jeans as he walked away from his last ride of the night. He had ridden Twister the full eight seconds and

31

was pretty darn satisfied that his ride had given him a good shot at second place. Stick Frye was the last bull rider on the line-up and he and Danny were neck and neck.

Stick had drawn a feisty young bull named Buzz Saw. Buzz had a reputation for changing directions in a heartbeat, but Stick was confident that he could finish this night off as a winner.

Boots had been unusually quiet the whole evening. As any father would have been on a night like this, and everyone chalked it up to nerves. Everyone but Marlene.

She kept glancing over at her husband every so often as he sat somberly on the bleachers next to Uncle Bud.

As Danny Douthitt walked out of the arena, Boots stood up and told Uncle Bud he was going down to the fence and get a closer look at Stick's next ride. Uncle Bud stood to go with him just as the announcement came over the loud speaker. It was Jim Shoulders.

"Well, folks, there's been a change of bulls for the last ride. Buzz Saw has been scratched and Stick Frye will now be seated on the back of none other than El Diablo. Comin' out of gate seven, is Stick Frye!" The crowd rose to their feet, the band began to play so loudly that no one but Marlene heard Boots yell at the top of his lungs, "STOP! STOP HIM! STOP!"

Marlene saw the look of sheer terror on Boot's face as he took three steps at a time down to the arena, with Uncle Bud running close behind.

Stick had complete control of his ride on El Diablo. The bull was putting on a tremendous show of twists and turns with Stick-tight Frye securely fastened high on its back. One hand on the rope and the other held high and mighty in the air, Stick Frye was a picture of showmanship

32

right up to the end of the ride. It was a magnificent ride. The eight-second buzzer rang loud and proud as El Diablo took one last leap high into the air. The crowd knew instantly that this ride had put Stick Frye into second place and the band struck up a rowdy rendition of "Cotton-Eyed Joe" as the people stomped and clapped, shouting "Stick! Stick! Stick!"

Boots Frye had scaled the fence and was halfway to reaching Stick and the bull when it happened. As El Diablo's back side came slamming down to the ground, Boots saw the animal's right hind leg sink and disappear into the muddy hole causing the 2,000-pound animal to flip up and back. Stick had been thrown off and had begun to prop himself up on his elbows as he looked behind his back and saw his dad running toward him.

"Roll away, Stick! Roll away!"

It was too late. When Stick turned his head back around, he looked up just in time to see El Diablo come crushing down on top of his chest.

Just like that. It was over.

CHAPTER 11:

Regret Is a Mighty Pill to Swallow

The paramedics slammed the gurney through the doors of the emergency room. Boots was running right beside his son talking to him the whole way down the hall to the second set of doors.

"I love you, son. I love you. Hang on. They're going to fix you right up. I'm right here, Stick, I'll never leave you."

"Mr. Frye, this is as far as you can go. We will be taking him back and they will let you know his condition as soon as possible."

Boots grabbed his son's hand one last time and gave it a big squeeze.

As he watched Stick being wheeled away, Boots put his face in his hands.

"I should have stopped him." He sobbed.

"What did you know, Boots? Tell me! I know you knew something." It was Marlene. Uncle Bud, Angie and Trey were standing in the hallway as Marlene charged toward her husband.

"Tell me!" She grabbed the front of his shirt with both hands and looked up at Boots.

"The nightmare. The nightmare came true, Marlene! I should have stopped him. In the dream, they substituted his bull for a bull named El Diablo. I should have stopped him." Boots' head went back as he squeezed his eyes shut.

Marlene commenced to beat Boots' chest with her fists. Over and over she struck his chest.

"Why didn't you tell me? We could have stopped him." She sobbed.

Boots pulled away from Marlene. "I have to get some air." He turned and ran down the hall, past Hannah, and her parents. Hannah fell down on her knees as Boots ran out the exit toward the parking lot.

"My God, my God! Why didn't I listen to you, God? You tried to tell me, and I didn't listen." Boots uttered aloud as he looked up into the heavens as if he were staring God right in the face.

Boots continued running beyond the parking lot into a field, hot tears streaking down his face, blurring his vision as he ran. Then he stopped right in his tracks.

"What am I doing? I can't be out here with him in there." Boots came to his senses as he suddenly teetered at the edge of an embankment. When he turned to go back to the hospital he began to lose his footing. His leather-soled boots slipped on the dewy grass and his fall backwards was swift and silent.

He never knew what hit him.

CHAPTER 12:

The Dream

Before Marlene could go after Boots, an emergency room physician came through the doors.

"Are any of you with the Frye family?"

"Yes, I'm his mother. How is my son?"

"He has lost a tremendous amount of blood, his pelvis is fractured, and his right arm and leg are shattered. We are taking him in to surgery right now." The doctor turned immediately to leave when Uncle Bud spoke up.

"What are his chances, doc?"

The doctor hesitated briefly, then spun around toward Marlene.

"If you are religious, then I would suggest you start praying now." He started to leave when he stopped again. "Oh, and whoever thought to put the tourniquet on that boy's arm will be credited with saving the kid's life. If he pulls through."

CHAPTER 12: THE DREAM

Marlene bolted toward the hospital exit. Her thoughts were racing as she looked all around to see if she could see any sign of her husband. When she ran out past the parking lot, she looked to her left and saw the glow of flashing lights at the bottom of an embankment. Three police cars and an ambulance were pulling up to the scene. As she stood at the top of the grassy ridge, looking down onto the street below, she saw Boots. He was lying in the street in a pool of blood.

She started to make her way down the slippery knoll as fast as she could go, stumbling and tripping as she went. As she stepped off the curb onto the street, an older gentleman rushed toward her. He looked at Marlene with fear in his eyes. "He came out of nowhere and landed right on top of my hood and when I slammed on the brakes he went flying off! Oh, my God! I didn't even see it was a person."

When Marlene reached Boots, she fell to her knees and crawled on top of him. She grabbed his face with both hands, turning it so he could look right into her eyes.

"Boots! Oh my God, Boots. Look at me, honey. Open your eyes and look at me. I'm right here, honey. Do you see me? Please nod and tell me you see me, Boots." His eyes slowly opened, as he tried to smile at her. A tear slid out of his eye and ran down her hand.

"Boots, you've got to listen to me. That dream you had. You and I both know that if you would have told me your dream I would have said it was just a stupid dream and our boy deserved his chance. Neither of us would have stopped him. Listen to me, Boots! We wouldn't have stopped him. The dream was for you to know that the bull's horn was going to go into his arm. You saved his life, honey! Boots, look at me! Boots, you saved Stick's life!"

He gave her one last tear streaked smile. He was gone.

CHAPTER 13:

Bad News Travels Fast

Uncle Bud arrived just in time to help Marlene up from on top of Boot's body. The front of her yellow sun dress was soaked in his bright, red blood. Tears would not come. They were both in complete shock at the tragic turn of events which had just shaped a humid Saturday night in northeastern Oklahoma. Bud put his arm around her shoulder and spoke clearly and gently. "Marlene, you need to be up there with Stick. You need to be there when he gets out of surgery. He's gonna need you now more than ever. Listen to me, Marlene, I'll take care of things here. I'll make sure they know Boots is going back to Tishomingo. I'll call Winston's and they can make the arrangements to come get him. Can you make it up that hill by yourself?"

Marlene squeezed Bud's forearm, nodded, then turned to make the climb up the grassy, slippery embankment. She didn't remember moving so fast in her life. She saw Angie and Hannah running toward her as she stepped up and onto the parking lot. A breathless Angie grabbed Marlene's hands. Their eyes met as she spoke. "Aunt Marlene, the doctor needs to talk to you right now. Oh, my Lord! What happened? You're covered in blood, Aunt Marlene. Where is Uncle Boots? This is all so unbelievable, Aunt Marlene."

Marlene Frye took off running toward the hospital at breakneck speed. "Come on girls, we've got to be with Stick!"

A surgical nurse was waiting for them as they rounded the corner in the hallway. She explained that there had been some complications and the doctor was wanting Marlene's permission to remove Stick's arm, if necessary. The paper was on a clipboard in the nurse's hand. There was a line for Marlene's signature glaring at her as her eyes met the paper.

"Miss, do you have children?" The blood-covered Marlene was calm and matter-of-fact as she looked up from the paperwork. Her question was directed toward the nurse.

"Yes, I have a son. Why?"

"If your boy was in that operating room right now would you trust his life to that surgeon?" Marlene looked at the nurse with a resolve only a mother would recognize.

"Yes, Mrs. Frye, without a doubt. He's the best in town. Probably, in the state."

"Okay, I am signing this paper and I want you to go back in there and tell the doctor that I trust him. Tell him I want him to do whatever he can to save my son." She was scribbling her signature across the page as she spoke.

Their eyes met as Marlene handed the clipboard back to the nurse. Nothing more needed to be said. The nurse turned and hurried toward the swinging doors leading back to the operating room. When Marlene wheeled around to continue down the hall, she couldn't help but feel as if she was in a slow-motion movie. People were gawking at her with their mouths wide open. The whispers were inaudible, but she knew instantly that they knew. They all knew this woman's son's life was hanging in the balance and she was standing there covered in blood because she had just witnessed the death of her husband in a very tragic accident. Bad news travels fast. Like lightning.

CHAPTER 14:

The Apparition

The surgical team was well-oiled and professional. They had been teaming up with Dr. Highsmith for several years and it was as if they knew what he was thinking before he spoke. They admired his skills and were proud to know that he requested their group to assist him on the most difficult cases. This particular surgery was going to need all of their attention. The poor kid lying on the operating table was mangled and crushed. By his chart, they could see he was only eighteen. Each individual standing in their position around Stick Frye in the operating room had thought to themselves that he had been very fortunate, or pretty darn lucky, to be truthful, to have Dr. Ben Highsmith as his surgeon. If anyone could piece this kid back together, it would be none other than Ben Highsmith. Dr. Highsmith was all business when he was performing a surgery and that's why what happened next had them all puzzled and alarmed.

"What's so funny? Who let that guy in here? Get him out immediately!" Dr. Highsmith looked up from his work and glared at the surgical team with a furrowed brow.

The startled surgical technicians and nurses began to look all around the room. What in the world was Dr. Highsmith talking about? They didn't see anyone. They hadn't heard anyone laughing. They looked at each other, with their eyes doing the talking over their masks. What the heck was up with Dr. Highsmith?

"Doctor, we don't see anyone."

"He's over there." Dr. Highsmith was visibly agitated as he spun around and pointed to the corner of the room.

"What? He's gone. Where did he go? There was a man standing over in the corner. He was laughing out loud. Are you telling me that none of you heard or saw him?" Dr. Highsmith was visibly agitated.

Eight heads very slowly went from side to side. No, they did not see a man standing in the corner of the operating room and they definitely had not heard any laughter. Was the surgeon feeling well? They were all frozen in their places not knowing what to do next. Should they ask him if he was okay? Should they go find someone and tell them that they thought there might be a problem with Dr. Highsmith?

If Dr. Highsmith hadn't had his surgical mask on they would have clearly seen him open his mouth to speak. He knew without a doubt what he had just seen. He had been startled by the outburst of the laughing and had looked up quickly enough to see the man standing in the corner only six feet away from the table. The cowboy had looked right at the surgeon and had given him a big "thumbs up".

"Are we ready to continue, everyone?" Dr. Highsmith knew he needed to get back to the business of saving Stick Frye's life…and limbs, but he was certainly very troubled by whatever had just transpired. Had he just seen an apparition?

CHAPTER 15:

The Farewell

Stick Frye heard his dad's voice. "Stick! Son, open your eyes! It's me."
Stick opened his eyes and looked around the operating room. His vision was blurry, and he strained to focus. He could see that he was in a hospital operating room. He could vaguely tell that he was being worked on by a surgeon. He could also see the team of surgical technicians and nurses as they moved about the room, handing instruments to the doctor, and removing blood-soaked gauze from the doctor's hand. His eyes focused on a figure that was standing right behind the doctor's left shoulder.

"Dad! Did you see my ride?"

"You bet I did, son! You took second place and it was your best ride ever!" Boots Frye laughed loudly as he spoke to Stick.

"It was my best ride ever, Dad. I loved every minute of it."

The surgical team, led by Dr. Highsmith, continued to work on Stick's mangled body. After Dr. Highsmith saw the cowboy in the operating

45

room it seemed to him that his hands were working at a frenzied pace. It was as if they were being propelled by an outside force. The surgeon had been dreading what he would find when he started to try to put Stick's arm back together. However, the moment he cut a slit near the punctured area every nerve seemed to go right back into place.

Boots began to look like a glowing figure standing in the operating room. "Stick, there's something I need to tell you, buddy. I'm getting ready here in a minute to go on to heaven. You know darn good and well that I would love to stay but that's not how the cards in my life were dealt. I want you to tell your mother that I will always love her with all my heart. You too, son, and it's going to be up to you to take care of her. You can do that for me. Can't you, Stick?"

"You bet I will, Dad." Stick tried to raise up from the operating table. "Please don't go." Stick began to cry as he reached for his dad.

At that moment, none other than the angel, Gabriel, appeared. Boots Frye was going to be escorted to heaven by Gabriel. What an honor! Stick knew his dad deserved it too.

"Wait one second, Dad! I have to tell you one last thing. Dad, tonight was not my best ride ever. My best ride ever was with you and Tooty Frooty." His dad shot him one last mile-wide grin.

Boots Frye's final ride was swift and magnificent. The glowing apparition disappeared into another dimension as Dr. Ben Highsmith left the operating room. The orthopedic team was on their way in to complete Stick's surgery.

The next thing Stick remembered was waking up in the recovery room.

"Milton. Wake up, Milton. I am your recovery room nurse, Gwen. Can you see me, Milton?"

Stick was so groggy. All he could see was that his entire body was in one huge cast, and the big lights above the bed were blinding him.

"Where's my mom? I want my mom. Please can I talk to my mom?"

"You're going to be in here for another thirty minutes before we take you to your hospital room. As soon as we feel like you can be moved, we will take you there. Your mom will be waiting for you." Nurse Gwen was busying around adjusting his IV fluids as she spoke.

"Please hurry. I need my mom now." Stick was no longer groggy as he raised his head to speak to the nurse.

CHAPTER 16:

Orchestrated by God

As soon as they wheeled Stick into his room, he pulled himself up on his one free elbow and looked around the room for his mom, Marlene.

"Mom!" he looked at her bloodstained dress and eased his head back. He knew instantly what he had experienced in the operating room was not just a dream. It had been orchestrated by God.

Tears streamed down Stick's temples as the nurse's aides moved him to his hospital bed. The pain he was experiencing by being jostled around paled in comparison to the pain in his heart. Marlene reached for her son's hand as soon as he was transferred from the gurney, and his IVs and monitors were situated at the head of his bed.

"Momma, I know dad is gone."

"How on earth do you know? Who told you, Stick?" Marlene was horrified at the thought that someone broke the awful news to her son without her permission.

As Stick began to speak, Dr. Highsmith entered the room.

"He came into the operating room to tell me goodbye. I know it was my dad. He was escorted to heaven by the angel Gabriel, Momma. I saw it with my own eyes!"

Dr. Highsmith's eyes grew as big as saucers.

"Mrs. Frye, do you happen to have a picture of your husband?"

Marlene pulled her wallet from her denim bag. When she popped open the snap and flipped through the pictures until she found her favorite one of Boots, she passed her wallet to the doctor.

Dr. Highsmith turned as white as a sheet as he gazed upon the photograph of the grinning cowboy. The same grinning cowboy had been standing in the operating room giving him "thumbs up".

"Oh, my God! That's him. I saw him. What the hell?" the bewildered surgeon let the wallet in his hand fall to the floor. His jaw dropped as he placed his hand over his mouth.

Dr. Highsmith had gone to church with his grandmother when he was a youngster, but he hadn't thought much about God since he became an adult. It was hard to reconcile his feelings about any kind of higher being when he had seen so much pain and suffering come through the doors of the operating room day after day. Ben Highsmith often felt so alone as he tried valiantly to piece his patients back together. 'Is there really a God?' That question loomed in his thoughts as he stood in Stick Frye's hospital room. He knew what he had seen. He knew without a doubt that Boots Frye had stood behind him as he operated on Stick. He also knew that Stick saw him too.

"I will be back. I need to make a phone call." Dr. Highsmith bent down and picked up Marlene's wallet from the floor. As he handed it back to her, he excused himself and slipped out of the room. The baffled doctor headed straight to his office, and locked the door behind him. He slid abruptly into his chair and twirled it around to look out the window, reaching for the telephone on his credenza. His brother, Paul, was a pastor of a small church in Wetumka, Oklahoma. They hadn't spoken in quite a while as Dr. Highsmith had grown weary of his brother's constant preaching to him about salvation and God, Jesus and faith, and all the other fairy tales…

"Paul, are you busy? I really need to talk to you." His voice began to crack as tears welled up in his eyes.

CHAPTER 17

Stick and Marlene Come to Grips

As much as he wanted to go, there was no way possible that Stick would be able to attend his father's funeral. He was still in intensive care, in a total body cast, and in need of around the clock care.

Hannah and Aunt Harriet stayed at the hospital in Tulsa with Stick, while Marlene, Uncle Bud and the rest of the family attended the memorial service for Ed "Boots" Frye.

The First United Methodist Church in Tishomingo, Oklahoma, was packed. Extra chairs had to be brought up from the basement to provide enough seating for all the people who had come to bid a final farewell to Boots Frye.

Jim Shoulders had made it a point to swing by the hospital in Tulsa to visit briefly with Stick before he headed to Tishomingo to attend the funeral. Rodeo folks stand together in triumph or tragedy and Marlene Frye was overwhelmed by the support.

One by one, the friends of Boots Frye took to the podium to share stories and condolences. It was a fine and fitting tribute to his legacy and it made Marlene proud to know that her husband was admired and loved by so many people.

At the conclusion of the service, Marlene insisted on hurrying back to Tulsa to be with her son. Her immediate prayer was for God to give her the strength to endure the road ahead as she realized she needed to stay strong for Stick. Only God knew what the future held for them both. In an instant, everything had changed.

When Marlene, Uncle Bud, Angie, and Trey arrived at Mercy General after Boots' funeral, they were met by Dr. Highsmith, who was standing outside the curtained-off area where Stick lay in intensive care.

"Mrs. Frye, I haven't had the chance to tell you how very sorry I am for the tragic turn of events in your family. I am so sorry that you have lost your husband, and that your son has lost his father. Words cannot express my sadness for you both. As hard as it is for you to hear, I must tell you that we are by no means out of the woods here with your son. He lost a tremendous amount of blood, which makes it a lot harder to fight back from the long and tedious surgery he has endured. The good news is that his body responded well to the transfusions, which will boost his immunity to try and fight off any infection that might attack his system. When he was transported here, his wounds were covered in mud. We did the best that we could in a life-threatening situation to cleanse him, but I'm not convinced that we were able to get rid of every microbial particle. Our immediate concern is infection. We will be giving him large dosages of antibiotics and will monitor him around the clock. The next 48 hours are crucial to his survival. I will be making rounds again this evening and will let the staff know that your family members are welcome to stay with him. Two at a time is the limit, but I believe that he will appreciate the support." He turned to leave, stopped, then looked directly into Marlene Frye's eyes before he walked away, "I will be praying for him."

Marlene stepped inside the curtained area. Stick was asleep. Her eighteen-year-old son looked five years old to her. Her heart sank as she saw all the tubes, monitors, bags, and IVs that were fastened onto and inserted into her boy. He could only lie on his back as the entire body, from the neck down, was left immobile due to the hard plaster cast that had him spread eagle and motionless.

"It wasn't supposed to be this way," she whispered.

Marlene had made a vow to herself on the drive back to Tulsa from Tishomingo. As many other resilient southern Oklahoma women before her had done as they faced their own hardships, Marlene Frye vowed to be strong for Stick. Crying and falling into a fetal position in the corner were not options. She had to buck up. Everything had changed in a moment in time and there was not one blasted thing she could do to put it back the way it was before. Boots was gone, and her only child lay broken and bruised in a cold, sterile hospital bed.

"Dear God, I need you now more than ever. Stick needs us both. You know I will do whatever it takes to get my boy back on his feet. He deserves to have a good life. I'm asking you to stay by my side and show me the way. I am totally at your mercy." It was a silent, fervent, necessary, heartfelt prayer. One of those kind that come up from the gut, down in the pit of one's soul that cries out to God for relief from the pain and suffering. The uncertainty for the future. The future. That was the number one concern at this moment in time. Stick deserved a future and Marlene was ready to fight for her son's life and his future.

"Stick, honey, it's momma. Are you hurtin' anywhere? Please let me know if you need anything or if you are hurtin'. I will not let you be in pain. Do you hear me, honey? You know your momma won't let you be in pain for one stinkin' minute. I will be hairy on ape at these nurses if they let you suffer." Stick began to stir as Marlene focused her attention on making sure every tube and IV was properly functioning. She rearranged the blankets on her son to make sure he was resting comfortably.

They were in this together. They would see this thing through. Marlene just knew it. She also knew she had the finest support group that could ever exist. Aunt Harriet had already been working on a schedule for the around-the-clock support for Stick. Uncle Bud had secured a motel room a few blocks from the hospital. It would be command central. They would sleep in shifts. Trey and Angie insisted that they be given their time slots to care for their beloved cousin. Hannah's parents had both called their employers to get vacation time to help in any way they could, and Hannah had not left Stick's side. Hannah would never leave Stick's side.

CHAPTER 18:

Some Broken Parts Don't Mend

Physical therapy was grueling. Even with Stick's determination to conquer the beast, there were days when he broke down in tears and told his therapists that he couldn't do it anymore. They would let him take a break to regain his composure, and like clock-work, he would get a second wind and continue until the session was completed. His progress was slow and steady though. In Stick's eighteen-year-old mind, slow and steady was a whole lot better than nothing at all.

Marlene and Hannah would take turns hanging out with him during his therapy sessions. Just having one of them nearby was very comforting and supportive. His two favorite women in the world were also his two favorite cheerleaders. He wanted them to be proud of him and that fact spurred him on when he would start to feel down.

The July heat in Oklahoma was sweltering, stifling, and quite unbearable to Marlene. Stick had completed his physical therapy session for the morning and he and his mom decided it was just too hot to eat in the outdoor patio of the nearby restaurant. They decided they were going to grab something from the hospital cafeteria and enjoy the air conditioning as long as they could. "Must be my old age catching up with me. I used to be able to handle the heat and humidity a lot better when I was younger." Marlene lamented as she stared out the window of the cafeteria. "Mom, you are not old. Stop that kind of talk right now. I see how those young doctors and maintenance guys look at you." Stick smiled his mile-wide grin at his blushing mother. She laughed out loud and threw her napkin across the table at her son. "Stop that foolishness right now!" They both chuckled as they finished their lunch.

Stick couldn't help but look at the nice-looking, young couple sitting at the table next to them. He had noticed them in the cafeteria on several other occasions, recalling that each time he saw them, the guy was savoring a piece of apricot pie. Stick never met a stranger and decided to be a nosy pie sleuth.

"You must really like apricot pie." Stick said as his and the guy's eyes met.

The young lady sitting with the "pie guy" started to laugh. "See, Larry, the word is out about you and your pie obsession!" Larry snickered, and his face turned beet red.

"Okay, folks, you found me out."

Marlene and Stick looked inquisitively at the young couple.

The woman spoke next. "Let me do the introductions. My name is Susan, and this is my fiancé, Larry. We work in the bank across the street. Larry is obsessed with hospital cafeteria food, especially the apricot pie. While other young couples are having romantic lunches over there at the Polo Grill, we have lunch on a regular basis in the cafeteria of Mercy General Hospital."

Stick laughed so hard he almost spit out his cheeseburger. Larry blushed, and Susan and Marlene shared knowing looks at each other.

"I wouldn't have him any other way though. He's a great guy." Susan reached over and patted Larry on his hand. His other hand was busy navigating a forkful of apricot pie toward his open mouth. "We have many romantic dinners in very nice restaurants all over Tulsa. If eating hospital cafeteria food for lunch makes him happy, well, I guess it makes me happy too!"

It felt good to laugh. Stick hadn't had much to laugh about in a while, so he didn't mind a bit if it was at Mr. Larry, the pie-eating banker's, expense.

Marlene glanced at her watch. They had twenty minutes until Stick's appointment with his neurosurgeon. It was to be the doctor's assessment of Stick's progress since he began his physical therapy. It had been an unspoken dread between Stick and his mom. Stick wanted to know what his future was going to look like. Would he ever regain all the strength in his arm and leg? Was the pain he dealt with every single day ever going to go away? He had already come to grips that he would never be able to rock and fire his famous cheese pitch or jettison his crazy knuckleball across home plate again. He would never hear the crowd cheer as he struck out player after player with his brushback pitch. He could knock 'em down like bowling pins but Stick knew that "could" was past tense. No more baseball. However, bull riding was a whole other story. The passion and drive were still there to straddle a bull way past the buzzer. Old El Diablo had not stolen that from him, that's for darn sure. It had been a very unfortunate accident. He knew it deep down inside, but he was hoping-against-hope that his doctor would tell him there was still a chance for him to ride bulls again. He was mentally preparing himself for any type of strength training that he would face to get that opportunity. He knew he would grab it by the horns.

Marlene, on the other hand, was mentally preparing herself for the words to come from the Dr.'s lips to their ears that Stick Frye had a very tough road ahead. Baseball and rodeo aside, she knew Stick's body had taken a horrible beating and the orthopedic and neurological surgical teams did their very best to piece him back together. What weighed heaviest on her mind were Stick's painful expressions. He tried so very hard to hide them from his mom and Hannah. The grimaces were what kept her awake at night. She knew he was suffering every day with pain and that's what scared her half to death. Her late husband, Boots, had been thrown from bulls practically his entire life. Name a bone and he had broken it. Many of them more than once. Boots had dealt with pain in the best way he knew how and that was what Marlene feared the most for her son.

The bottle. It had almost ruined their marriage in the early years. Boots had been determined not to get hooked on pills and Marlene had begged him to try to find a good doctor to help him with his pain. He hated doctors and called them quacks. If Marlene started "harpin' on him about findin' a doctor," Boots Frye closed his ears defiantly to that suggestion. Like many busted and broken bull riders before him, he had already found solace without making an appointment. His "clinic" was on the outskirts of the town. Wet Yer Whistle Liquors was open 24/7. No appointment was necessary, and Marlene always knew when Boots' pain was unbearable. He would come home from work carrying a bottle of whiskey with the tell-tale paper sack twisted around its neck. He wouldn't and couldn't look her in the eye. They both knew that it was not going to be a good night. Before Marlene would head to bed alone, she would peek through the window blinds. Boots would be in the porch swing with his head tilted back, eyes closed, the half empty bottle of Jack in his hand. She could hear him as he sat on the back porch until the wee hours, singing old rodeo songs and talking to the bottle. She loathed his favorite Mark Twain quote, "Too much of anything is bad, but too much good whiskey is barely enough." She would quietly close the blinds when the tears started to fall, and they wouldn't be her tears.

As Marlene fidgeted nervously with her purse, she and Stick waited anxiously for the nurse to take them back to talk to the doctor. The memory that popped into her head at that moment was the day she packed a picnic lunch and she and Boots went to her uncle's heated dock on Lake Texoma to fish for crappie.

Her marriage to Boots took one sentence to save. Before he dropped his worm-covered hook into the cold waters of the lake, Marlene placed her hand on his and looked directly into his eyes, "Boots, I'm pregnant and if you don't stop drinking, I'm leaving you and never coming back."

The main thing Boots knew about his wife, Marlene, was that she didn't bluff. Ever. That's all it took. He was stone sober in a heartbeat, and his new physician, Dr. Merton, not only helped control his pain, but became his best friend and fishing buddy.

"Milton Frye, you and your mother can come back now." They sighed in unison as they arose from their seats to follow the nurse beyond the waiting room door.

CHAPTER 19:

The Road to Somewhere

At Marlene's request, Uncle Bud Looper had written letters to every college that had been scouting his nephew. He thanked them profusely for the interest they had shone in Stick and explained that the injuries he had suffered in the accident had permanently ended his baseball career. In response, the letters from the colleges were heartfelt and sincere. Each athletic director expressed their disappointment that Stick Frye would not be able to continue his quest for a spot on their respective college baseball teams. They wished him success and happiness for his future endeavors, leaving their inked signature in the left-hand corners of each embossed page. Several even enclosed team ball caps. There had been debates as to the effect of that gesture. Would the caps make him feel worse or would they make him proud of his accomplishments that had led up to the moment in time that the clock stopped forever? They chose to go for the latter. Stick Frye could someday show the caps to his children and grandchildren and reminisce about the "good old days."

The prognosis Stick and Marlene received from the neurosurgeon on that day was devastating. Stick was lucky to be alive, and for that they were both grateful to God above, but the rest was gut-wrenching. There was nothing more to be done for Stick. He had reached maximum recovery. No hope for any more feeling to return. None. Through tears, Marlene asked the doctor about the pain. Stick turned his head away from his mom and the doctor to hide his disappointment. He couldn't suppress his tears as the doctor explained that pain management would be an ever-present part of Stick's future. For a moment, he felt like he was free-falling into a bottomless pit. Nausea and despair...only for a moment, though. Stick Frye was the son of Boots and Marlene Frye. Enough said.

Self-pity never for one moment entered the mind of Stick Frye. He was the son of the toughest parents he had ever known. Stick knew that his dad, Boots, would never let him wallow in pity of any kind. Boots always said, "We were put on this earth for one go 'round. Just one. There are no overs, but we can always darn sure pick ourselves up, dust ourselves off, and start all over again."

That's exactly what Stick was determined to do.

CHAPTER 20

A New Path

Stick and Hannah's new plan was to get married at the end of summer. The original early June date had been changed after the accident. Stick wanted time in therapy, so he could make sure that he could dance the two-step at his wedding to his beautiful and precious bride. Everyone knew Stick would dance with Hannah at their wedding. If Stick set his mind to something, it happened. Come hell or high water.

Furthermore, since he was at square one, career wise, Stick was happy to get a visit from his Tishomingo High School guidance counselor. He had just finished a grueling and painful physical therapy session and was glad to have a break to talk to his visitor, Mr. Hankins.

Mr. Hankins had brought Stick's high school file with him. They went to the cafeteria of the hospital to eat some lunch and talk about possible options for Stick.

"Stick, when I was looking through your file, I noticed that you had expressed an alternative choice for a career path. I show where you listed farming as something that you had an interest in doing. Do you think you might still have a passion for something like that?"

"I sure do, Mr. Hankins. I would love to farm."

"That's great, son. Here is the contact information for an old college friend of mine. We went to Oklahoma State University together. He is heading up the agriculture program over at NEO A&M, in Miami, Oklahoma, and his name is Harry Synar. I will give him a call and let him know you might be getting in touch with him if you'd like."

"Yes, please do that, Mr. Hankins. It sounds like a good plan for me. I will talk to Hannah about it and if it sounds good to her, I will give him a call. Thank you so much for coming all the way over to Tulsa to see me and thanks so much for your help."

"It's my pleasure, Stick. You have always been a great student and I know wherever you go in life, you will represent Tishomingo in the finest way. You know I thought the world of your father. I'm sure going to miss our fishing trips to Lake Texoma. Nobody could bring in the stripers like Boots Frye. I hear your mom is moving to Broken Arrow to be close to her cousin and her family. That sounds like a great plan for her. You know I wish you both the best and I'm so sorry this all happened, but you and Marlene are survivors. I have no doubt you both will come out of this on top."

CHAPTER 21:

Hannah and Stick Get Hitched

The wedding was sweet and upbeat. Trey Looper served as Stick's best man. Jill McEntyre, Hannah's best friend, was her maid of honor, and Angie Looper was one of three bridesmaids. Since the accident, Hannah's relationship with the Loopers had blossomed and Hannah was excited that she and Angie were going to be in the same family. It was a marriage made in heaven as far as everyone was concerned.

The moment Hannah entered the sanctuary on the arm of her father, she saw him. Stick was standing in the aisle looking directly at Hannah. His injured leg was jutted out to the side, held motionless by a stiff brace. His right arm was in a white cotton sling. She immediately noticed that he had written "Stick and Hannah Forever" in bright red letters on the front of the sling. In his left hand he held a microphone. It was impossible for Hannah to hold her composure when the music started, and Stick began to sing to his beautiful bride. It was "My Love" by Sonny James.

As Stick continued to sing, Hannah turned to her father, lifted her veil, and gave him a big kiss on the cheek. "Here I come, Stick!" With a mile-wide grin on both of their faces, Hannah proceeded to run the rest of the way down the aisle. Straight to Stick.

There were no pomp and circumstances to their ceremony, it was just a simple and pure example of "we love each other so let's get this show on the road".

JoJo Riley closed the ceremony with a heartfelt rendition of "We've Only Just Begun" as the bride and groom turned and faced each other. Stick grabbed Hannah's trembling hand with his one good hand and gently wiped away tears of joy from her cheeks with the cotton sling on his other. They knew they were in this for the long haul.

"Ladies and gentlemen, it's my pleasure to introduce to you, Mr. and Mrs. Stick-Tight Frye!" Uncle Bud held open the door to the fellowship hall as Stick escorted his new bride into the room.

The reception was filled with music and fun, and to the amazement of the onlookers in the reception hall, Stick pulled off the perfect First Dance two-step (perfect to them, that is). Stick and Hanna shuffled their way around the dance floor, to Ronnie Milsap's "Pure Love", never taking their eyes off each other.

They were man and wife, for the good times and the bad. Through thick and a whole lot of thin, Hannah and Stick Frye were ready to tackle life together. Come what may….

CHAPTER 22:

College and Married Life

M r. Hankins relayed to Stick and Hannah that NEO A&M in Miami, Oklahoma, was delighted to welcome the newlyweds to their campus. Mr. Hankins' friend, Harry Synar, had taken a look at Stick's high school transcript and expressed his anticipation to get Stick signed up for NEO's agricultural classes.

Hannah loved designing her own clothes, so she was thrilled to see that NEO had a great fashion merchandising course of study, coincidentally under the direction of Bonnie Synar, Harry Synar's wife. Things were amazingly falling into place for the young couple as they moved into married housing on the college campus in Miami.

Miami (pronounced My-Am-Uh) sat smack dab in the far northeastern corner of Oklahoma. It boasted a steady population of around 14,000 people, the number one rated junior college in the nation in football, a Little League baseball program that qualified a team for the Little League

World Series each year, and a church on every corner. It was small town America at its very finest. Stick and Hannah loved it from the very first time they dined on hamburgers and cherry-vanilla Dr. Peppers at the The KuKu. What's not to love about a place that had a drive-in named The KuKu?

They had never seen anything like the KuKu in Tishomingo, or Madill, for that matter. The first time they dined there was on a Friday night, and Stick and Hannah figured out pretty quickly that it was the place to be for the teens in Miami. As they enjoyed their meal, they saw car after car of teenage drivers pull into the drive-in hamburger joint. The cars would circle around the back of the place and come around to the south side, hoping to find an empty parking spot that they could back their cars into and begin the nightly ritual of sitting in or on their cars, sneaking gulps of beer, puffs of cigarettes, socializing with all the cool kids and laughing their buns off at the newly licensed drivers, as they struggled clumsily to back their cars into the parking places right in front of God and everybody. It was very cheap entertainment for Stick and Hannah on their tight, newlywed budget.

Stick and Hannah had a ritual most weekends. They went to the KuKu on Friday nights, and if they could muster up one dollar on Saturday nights, they would pop a paper sack full of buttered popcorn, throw a blanket in their car and head to the Sooner Drive-In, where they would lie on the blanket and watch movies under the stars. Most weekends, that is. Unless the pain was just too unbearable…

CHAPTER 23

Up North

Hannah was chosen to travel to Dallas with a group of fashion merchandizing students from NEO to attend the Dallas Market for a three-day weekend. It was the first time in their marriage that she and Stick would be apart, and Hannah was worried sick that she wouldn't be there to take care of him if he had one of his bad spells.

"Honey, I have everything written down for you right here on this pad. If the pain gets to be unbearable, take three of the aspirins every four hours. Don't forget to use your ice packs and the heating pad is plugged in and ready here by the couch. I will try to find a pay phone, so I can check on you, and if you are feeling good, please go and do something fun. Isn't there a rodeo up north in Baxter Springs, Kansas? Didn't I hear Dooley and Spoon talking about it yesterday?"

Ben Dooley and Howie Spoon were Stick's new friends from college. They were all on NEO's Meat Judging Team together.

"Yeah, babe, there is one. I was thinkin' about goin' up there. I'd love to watch some bull ridin'. I'm feelin' pretty good today, just a little bit of soreness in my leg but otherwise I'm good."

Hannah gave Stick one last tender kiss and headed out the door to gather with the fashion merchandizing group for the five-hour drive to Dallas, Texas.

Baxter Springs, Kansas was just up and over the Oklahoma state line. Most of the locals referred to the trek to Baxter as "goin' up north".

As backing cars into a parking spot at the KuKu was a rite of passage for the local high school kids, "goin' up north" was a rite of passage for under-age drinkers in the northeastern corner of Oklahoma. Twenty-one was the legal age to drink in Oklahoma, but Kansas allowed drinking at the tender age of eighteen. It was an endless ribbon of cars heading up north on the weekends from Miami. Most of them were college students from NEO.

Dooley and Spoon called and invited Stick Frye to travel up north with them. They mentioned playing pool in a place called Kapler's, in Baxter, or going on to Galena, Kansas to listen to a band at a bar called The Ranch, then ending up at the rodeo to watch bull riding. It all sounded fun to Stick so he agreed to tag along.

When he heard the clanking noises of Spoon's old truck pull up to his apartment, Stick hurriedly gulped down three aspirins, set his glass of strawberry Kool-Aid down on the kitchen counter and proceeded to put the little tin of pills in the front pocket of his jeans. Both his leg and his arm had started to throb a bit earlier in the afternoon, so Stick was trying his darnedest to stay ahead of the pain.

Ben Dooley had his big ol' head sticking out of the passenger side of Spoon's truck. A toothy grin was plastered all over his face, and he was wearing a black, open crown cowboy hat with a large turkey feather sticking up and out of the hat band. Spoon laid on the horn as Stick walked toward the truck, just to be ornery.

Dooley scooted to the middle, Stick piled in, and they were headed up north.

CHAPTER 24:

Road Hog at the Ranch

"Hey, Stick, wanna sip of some Wild Turkey?" The three strapping young men filled the seat of Spoon's truck to the brim. Dooley, sitting in the middle, had to straddle the gear shifter that stuck straight up from the floorboard of the truck, making his knees flare outward, crowding out Stick's and Spoon's legs. When he reached down, pulled up the pant leg of his jeans, stuck his hand into his cowboy boot to flash the half pint of whiskey, Spoon yelled, "Doo! You're gonna make me wreck my truck, buddy! Get your knee back outta the way."

Dooley laughed, unscrewed the lid, and took a big swig of the whiskey.

"Stick, this'll light a fire under your tail. Want some?"

Stick kindly refused the offer to imbibe. There had never been a drop of alcohol in the Frye house as long as Stick could remember. His dad, Boots, lambasted the evil concoction on a daily basis. "Son, it just ain't worth the misery. Alcohol is straight from the devil's cauldron, that's for sure, and I highly recommend that you steer clear from it ever landin' on your lips. It can be a home-wrecker."

"No thanks, Dooley. I'd better not." Stick replied as he looked out the window of the truck, wishing and hoping that the pain shooting down his leg would go away.

"What the heck?" Stick turned and looked at Spoon and Doo. "What are those?" Off in the distance were humongous piles of some type of small rock rising like mountains on the horizon.

"Those are chat piles. I heard they used to mine for lead and zinc around here and that's the waste that was rejected in the mining operations. Doo and I came over here with some local guys from Miami a couple of weeks ago and snuck up on some girls skinny dippin'. There's all kinds of pools of water around there. That was a fun night." Spoon laughed and winked at his passengers.

"It sure was a real fun night!" Doo's eyes lit up when he seconded Spoon's analogy of the memory of their previous excursion as Spoon pulled his truck into the parking space near Kapler's.

They strolled into Kapler's and immediately spotted some of their other friends from NEO, over in the corner of the bar. The young men were playing pool and drinking beer and when they saw Stick, Doo and Spoon enter the bar, they motioned for them to come and join them in a game of pool.

Spoon and Doo bought themselves Coors beers and Stick asked for an Orange Crush. The bartender told him that all they had was Coke or Bubble Up, so he settled for the Bubble Up. It had only been thirty minutes since he had taken the three aspirins, but Stick didn't think it would hurt, and Hannah wasn't there, so he reached into the front pocket of his jeans, pulled out the tin of aspirins, opened it up and looked at the small white pills. Stick grabbed five and washed them down with the Bubble Up.

After three games of pool and shooting the breeze with their friends, Spoon asked Stick and Dooley if they were ready to go to The Ranch. Spoon had heard earlier in the week that a good band was going to be playing. They were a hard-hitting rock band called Road Hog.

It was a unanimous decision to leave Kapler's and head to Galena to The Ranch. Stick told himself that the five aspirins would be kicking in soon, as he limped out the door of the bar and cautiously climbed into the pickup truck with his friends.

The short drive to Galena, Kansas had them pulling into the parking lot of the large barn-like structure in plenty of time to get through the doors before the band started.

"Stick, are you okay? You haven't said much, and I saw you limpin' out of Kapler's." Spoon had jumped out of the driver's side of his truck and hurried over to open the passenger side door before Stick could get out.

"Oh, man. I'm sorry. I sure don't want to put a damper on our night, but my leg is hurtin' really bad tonight. I'm thinkin' about just staying out here in the truck."

"No way, Stick. We're not leavin' you out here. We can go back to Miami. It's no problem at all to take you back and I mean it." Spoon was sincere as he placed his hand on Stick's shoulder.

"I shouldn't have come in the first place. It was throbbin' some before we left. I feel bad for taggin' along now."

Dooley reached down for the whiskey in his boot. "Stick, I promise you this will make you feel better. Just for tonight. Just drink some and it will take the edge off your pain and you can relax and listen to the band."

The guilt that Stick felt for messing up the fun for Dooley and Spoon outweighed any guilt that he had for going against his dead father's dire warnings. Stick held his hand out for the bottle, screwed off the cap, and proceeded to take a long, slow draw of the amber liquid. It was hot going down his throat but when no demons came to scoop him up and fly away with him, Stick decided to give it another go. The second gulp went down smoother.

"Let's go in." Stick wiped his mouth with the back of his hand, gave the bottle back to Doo, and the three young men found themselves in the line to pay their cover charge. The burly guy at the door took their money and stamped the trio's left hands, giving them full access to the bar.

The place was packed. Stick was starting to feel a nice, warm glow from the effects of the alcohol, and realized how badly he was missing Hannah. "I will have to bring her here. We would have fun." He thought to himself.

The band was very good. Spoon and Doo, both single, found several cute college girls and danced the night away. Stick, on the other hand, woke up on the couch in his apartment the next morning with no memory of the night before, past walking into The Ranch. He still had his clothes on, and he was pretty sure that his friends were the ones that helped him take off his boots. His head was pounding, and he was extremely nauseous. What the heck had happened?

His thoughts were interrupted by the loud ring of the telephone hanging on the wall in the kitchen. It took him a couple of tries to get up off the couch.

"Hello, baby!" It was Hannah. She sounded so sweet and cheerful. "I have enough quarters to talk about three minutes, honey. How are you?"

"Hello, darlin'." It took everything in him to talk. He was so nauseous. "I'm just fine and I don't want to spend three minutes talkin' about me. I want to hear everything you've been doin'. Fill me in, sugar."

Stick was so glad that Hannah didn't catch on to the fact that he was "under the weather". He sat at the kitchen table with his head in his hand as she proceeded to tell him how much fun she was having and how much she was learning on her trip. As much as he adored his precious wife, he was never more relieved when he heard the operator break into their conversation, informing Hannah that she needed to deposit more money if she wanted the call to continue.

"We're heading back out now, and I love you…" she was cut off after she didn't deposit another quarter.

"Ughhh. I love you too, Hannah." Stick groaned to himself after he placed the receiver back in its cradle. He was face down on the table, fighting the urge to run to the bathroom and put his face smack dab into the toilet. His mouth was beginning to water.

When he decided there was nothing he could do to keep from feeling like the room was spinning, there was a light knock on the door. Stick immediately understood the futility of trying to stand up to see who was there.

"I see you're off the couch where we left you." It was Spoon and Doo. They hadn't locked the door behind them when they deposited Stick on his couch a few hours earlier, so they came on in and stood in the doorway to the kitchen. They didn't look much better than he felt.

"What happened to me? I feel like I've been hit by a freight train."

Dooley explained to Stick that they gotten hammered at The Ranch. Stick had started to feel better after the swigs of the Wild Turkey. A whole lot better. They had continued to drink throughout the evening. Spoon and Doo danced, and Stick sat at the table and enjoyed the music. Unfortunately, none of them remembered the drive back to Miami. Spoon was relieved that he hadn't been pulled over by the cops. Well, he presumed he had been the driver.

"One thing I can say, Stick, is your pain went away. Just like I told ya it would do," Dooley sheepishly announced as Stick found one of his school books on the kitchen table and threw it at his friend. Dooley was able to catch it before it hit his leg. He knew he probably deserved to be hit by the flying book, but he stood by his point. Stick's pain subsided when he got drunk.

CHAPTER 25:

A Toe in the Water

It took Stick the rest of the weekend to recover from the Friday night fiasco with Spoon and Dooley. He ate a few saltine crackers here and there but was relieved to notice he was finally getting his appetite back when his Hannah walked through the door.

"Hi, Hannah, my beautiful sweetheart. I'm so glad you're home safe. I missed you so very much."

Hannah dropped her suitcase just inside the doorway of their apartment and ran straight into Stick's waiting arms. They held each other for a long time. Hannah's embrace was joyful and passionate. Stick's was joyful, and guilt ridden. He had naively vowed to himself to never touch another drop of alcohol again and he wanted to just forget the whole event. Not telling Hannah made him feel a bit guilty, but he reasoned with himself that telling Hannah could be a whole lot worse than a twinge of guilt.

"You look a little pale, honey." Hannah stepped away from Stick's embrace with a furrowed brow after she took a good look at him. "Are you okay? Did you have a bad pain spell this weekend? Please tell me you didn't. If you did and I wasn't here to take care of you, I…"

Stick lovingly placed his finger on her lips.

"Now, shush, Hannah. I don't want to have any of that talk. I'm so glad you got to go on this trip and there's not gonna to be any talk about how in the heck I feel or don't feel. I'm probably pale because I missed you." He pulled her back into his arms for another hug.

"Okay, babe, I'll go fix us some dinner." Hannah kissed him on the cheek and headed toward the kitchen.

"I can't wait to hear all about Dallas." Stick said to Hannah as she walked away. He knew he just told a fib. What he couldn't wait to do was find out where he had to go to buy just a small bottle of whiskey. He told himself that having just a small bit of it around couldn't hurt. If it could ease his pain, he couldn't see the harm.

CHAPTER 26:

Slip Slidin' Away

"Southern Fried is playin' at The Ranch Saturday night," Spoon was cinching up the saddle of the horse he would be riding to check the cattle. Spoon and Stick had both gotten work study jobs at the NEO A&M College Farm. It was located northeast of the college. Stick was loving the farm life so much so that he knew he was on the right path. It would be hard, but satisfying work. Just like baseball or bull ridin'.

For two long weeks, Stick had been fighting the devil that seemed to have made a permanent home smack dab on his shoulder. The urge to drink was strong but having Hannah home had been a tremendous relief. She kept him supplied with aspirins, cold packs, and the heating pad. Lots of tender loving care from his precious bride had helped.

However, that devil often interrupted his thoughts about Hannah. "Just one drink to ease the pain, Stick. Why on earth would you want to suffer when a little bit of whiskey would do the trick?"

Thinking about the possibilities of a fun night at The Ranch with Hannah, helped Stick chase the nagging devil away on this sunny afternoon at work on the farm with Howie Spoon.

"You know, that sounds fun, Spoon. I've been tellin' Hannah that I want to take her there. You should go ahead and ask the Synar's cute daughter if she can go." Stick said with a wink.

Spoon's face turned a thousand different shades of red.

The Synar family lived on the College Farm. The two agriculture students would cut sideways glances toward the house when Harry and Bonnie Synar's youngest daughter, Susan, would pull her car into the driveway. She was a knockout.

"She's in high school!" Spoon looked at Stick like he was crazy as he jumped up into the saddle, slapped the reins on the horse's side, mumbling as the unsuspecting steed plodded forward, "She's too young to go to The Ranch and she definitely is way outta my league. She wouldn't look twice at me. Once would scare her off."

Stick laughed out loud at his funny friend. He was already getting excited to ask Hannah if she wanted to go to The Ranch on Friday. Even the normally bumpy ride in the Synar's old Willy's Jeep didn't seem so bad that day.

He couldn't wait to ask Hannah.

Spoon invited a girl from Vian, Oklahoma, to go with him to see Southern Fried. He was shocked that such a cute girl said yes to him. Little did he know that a lot of the incoming freshmen girls at NEO had their sights set on Howie Spoon. Humility kept him sweet, and he had no earthly idea that the girls swooned as they walked behind him in the hallways. Barbie Stonewall, from Vian, was attending NEO on a scholarship to be a Norse Star. The Norse Stars were NEO's performing dance team. It would be a sea of envy in tiny uniforms and cowgirl hats when Barbie would tell all the other girls at practice that spending time with Howie Spoon was part her weekend plans.

Friday night came and the four of them piled into Stick and Hannah's car as the two couples headed up north.

The band was so good even Stick made it to the dance floor with Hannah. They were having a wonderful time. Hannah knew Barbie, Spoon's date, from one of her classes at NEO. It always helps when there's a double date and the girls click.

Hannah excused herself to go stand in the long line to the restroom, and the line seemed to be moving very slowly. She suspected there could possibly be some girls struggling to get up from the toilet or stumbling as they tried to fasten their jeans. Lots of alcohol was being consumed in the bar and she had seen her share of weaving patrons.

As she made her way closer to the entrance to the bathroom, Hannah recognized some people from NEO. One guy had her perplexed though. He looked familiar. Was it possibly that Jack guy that worked at Farrier's grocery store in Miami?

Her train of thought was interrupted when she glanced toward the bar. Stick and Spoon were standing there. Her eyes landed on Stick's hand. He was holding a glass of beer. Was it for Barbie? She had never seen Stick with a beer. Or for that matter, she had never seen Stick near any alcohol at all.

"Babe, was the line long? I almost came to rescue you." Stick had a big grin on his face as Hannah made her way back to their table.

"It was a mad house over there. Two girls almost got into a fist fight. Kinda reminded me of Granny's two banty roosters." Hannah laughed as she sat down beside Stick.

"Stick, are you drinking that beer?" Hannah whispered into Stick's ear.

"Just this one, honey. I thought I would try a beer. Spoon said he'd buy me the next one if I like it." He laughed as he lifted the glass up to his lips. Hannah did not know that Stick had already been sneaking drinks of whiskey the entire night.

Hannah's parents were social drinkers, keeping it low key, strictly on the nights they and their friends gathered at each other's homes for Bridge night. Harvey Wallbangers, Rob Roys, and Tequila Sunrises. Quite the contrary, Stick's house was always alcohol free. Stick often told Hannah that Boots Frye hated booze. He never went into much detail about it, but she knew that Stick had never been around drinking in his life. Even the hard-core rodeo bull riders knew that Stick and his dad always steered clear of alcohol.

"Okay, Stick." Hannah smiled a sweet smile and gave Stick's hand a quick squeeze. She trusted him implicitly. He had never done anything to make her feel differently. He had always made good, sound decisions. They were just having a fun night. That's what she told herself. Her naivety blinded her from seeing that her husband was slowly slip slidin' away...

CHAPTER 27:

The Night in the ER

Hannah and Barbie were talking about the great music they had been enjoying, and Stick and Spoon were talking about the upcoming meat judging contest coming up in Fort Scott, Kansas. Fort Scott was the team to beat. Stick raised his glass of beer to drain the last drop from the clear, glass mug as the golden liquid dripped into the cupped area of his tongue.

"Stick! What's wrong? Oh my God!" Hannah jumped up from her seat, placing her hands over her mouth.

Stick had dropped the mug in mid-air. It came bouncing loudly down on the table.

"I can't breathe, Hannah. My throat's closin' up!" Stick gasped as he held his hands up to his throat. His eyes were as big as silver dollars.

Spoon jumped up from the table. His chair fell backwards on the floor as he took off running toward the bar. People were beginning to come over to the table to see if there was anything they could do to help Stick.

87

After listening to Spoon's urgent plea for help for his friend, the bartender spun around to the telephone behind the bar and called a local ambulance. He assured Spoon that the ambulance was on the way.

The time seemed to drag on and on, but in reality, the ambulance made it to the bar in four minutes. They had Stick strapped on a gurney in seconds flat and headed out the door with Hannah, Spoon, and Barbie close behind.

The local ER had been alerted in advance, therefore there was no waiting. The paramedics busted the gurney through the swinging doors and the medical team took over from there.

Spoon had driven Stick and Hannah's car at breakneck speed following as close behind the ambulance as he could. He had quite a buzz at the bar but found that he was sobering up quickly as he spun the car into a nearby parking spot. Hannah jumped out and was halfway inside the ER entrance before Spoon fully had the vehicle in park.

They were in for a long night.

After poking, prodding, urinalyses, and vials of blood, they let Hannah know the results. He was allergic to beer. Stick Frye had had a severe allergic reaction to the beer that he drank at The Ranch. Severe enough that his throat and his eyes had swollen almost shut.

"Mrs. Frye, you can come in and see your husband now." The nurse popped her head out of the door to the waiting room and motioned for Hannah to follow her back to the area where they had been treating Stick. It was four in the morning. He looked up at Hannah with swollen slits for eyes.

"I am so sorry, Hannah. I feel so stupid. I can't believe I ruined our date by drinking that stupid beer. I had no idea."

"Honey, you didn't know you were allergic to it. Now we know, and you are fine. Thank God for that."

CHAPTER 28:

No Beer for Stick

Stick and Hannah settled into married life and college life. Everything, as far as Hannah knew, was back to normal.

At least for a few days.

They both had been studying for mid-term exams. Hannah had a study group that met in the commons area of one the dorms. The dorms at NEO were not co-ed, therefore Hannah met her friends in an all-girl building by the large fountain due east of the administration building.

Stick, Spoon, and Dooley, were studying together also, that is after a quick trip across the state line. There was a liquor store at the edge of where Miami, Oklahoma and Seneca, Missouri met. It was called State Line Liquors and was directly across the street from the evaporated milk plant with the large storage container which was painted to look like an enormous can of Milnot.

She looked down at her watch and saw that it was ten pm. Hannah gathered up her books, said goodbye to her study partners, and headed home. She felt good about her mid-term exams and Stick had promised to meet her at their house with a carry-out pizza. Hannah was hoping that he got pepperoni, her favorite.

Hannah Frye knew something was wrong as soon as she walked up and heard loud music coming from their apartment. The front door wasn't closed all the way. It opened easily with just a gentle push and she immediately saw there weren't any lights on anywhere. As she set her purse and books down on the little table by the front door, Hannah's eyes became adjusted to the dark. Upon entering her home, she saw that Dooley was passed out on the couch. Spoon was over by the record player, holding up a flashlight, flipping through Stick and Hannah's albums looking for the next selection to play. He looked startled when he noticed Hannah standing in the living room.

"Where's Stick?" Hannah's short inquiry startled Spoon. He glanced toward the kitchen and attempted to speak. Unfortunately for Stick, Hannah didn't have to wait long for the answer to her question. She heard her husband and a female laughing and it was coming from the kitchen. A fuming Hannah found the light switch and pushed it in the upward position.

"Hi, Hannah, I'm teaching Barbie how to do the two-step." Stick was obviously very drunk, and Howie's girlfriend, Barbie, was in no better condition. They both smiled sheepishly toward Hannah, but Hannah was not smiling back. The two dancers were stumbling and hanging off each other as Hannah's eyes landed directly on the placement of Barbie's left hand. Barbie was securely grasping the right cheek of Stick's butt.

Hannah purposefully turned the light off, walked toward the door, picked up her purse and left.

CHAPTER 29

The Harsh Realities of Life

Stick woke up the next morning lying face down on the kitchen floor. He pulled himself up into a sitting position and sat there for a few seconds until he could figure out where he was. He had a very sinking feeling in his stomach and it had nothing to do with his horrible hangover. He had a flashback of Hannah standing in the doorway of the kitchen, and he was dancing with Barbie. He remembered the look on Hannah's face just before she turned the light off. Stick immediately grabbed the seat of the nearest kitchen chair, hoisted himself up as fast as he could with his bum leg, and headed toward the living room. Spoon and Barbie were sound asleep and cuddled together on the couch. Dooley was sprawled across Stick and Hannah's bed, snoring like a freight train. Stick bolted out the door and ran toward the parking area as fast as he could. Hannah's car was gone. He looked at his watch and knew that she had had time to drive to Madill.

Hannah refused to take Stick's calls. Her father told him, in no uncertain terms, that Stick needed to leave her alone, so she could sort things out in her head.

That's the very last thing that Stick wanted to hear. He woke the sleeping trio and told them in the nicest way possible to immediately get the heck out of his house.

After a very quick shower, he jumped in his truck and headed south to Madill. It was a solid four-hour drive but he was hoping he could shave that down to three. If he drove ninety he could do it. He drove ninety.

Stick saw Hannah's car in her parents' driveway. There was another car parked beside it. He almost swallowed his tongue when he recognized whose car it was that was parked beside Hannah's. He was in for it, that's for sure. He would rather tangle with a rattlesnake. There in the driveway sat a car, right next to Hannah's. "Lord, help me." He sighed. The car next to Hannah's, was his mom's. Marlene Frye was inside the Kimball's house, waiting for her son to show up on the doorstep. She knew he would be there and she was right.

Stick's hand was trembling when he knocked lightly on their front door. He heard footsteps. Next, came the sound of the knob slowly turning. It was like the gate lowering over a castle moat when the door deliberately opened to reveal Hannah's father standing solemnly in the doorway. He didn't smile, but Stick was encouraged by the fact that he didn't yell at him.

"Morning, Stick. Hannah's in the den."

If Stick Frye thought that the walk to a bucking chute to mount a monster bull was an arduous task, the slow walk to the den to face Hannah and his mom, seemed like an eternity. He was thinking about how a prisoner felt when he trudged his way to the gallows...

Hannah was sitting on a footstool. The Kimball's old red setter was standing in front of her with his face in her lap and Hannah was gently stroking his furry head.

Marlene Frye was standing behind the couch with her arms crossed. The minute Stick entered the room, their eyes locked, and he knew instantly that she was extremely disappointed in her son. He felt awful.

"Sit down, Stick. Momma, can you and Marlene please go on in the kitchen and leave Stick here with me, so we can talk?"

The two mothers readily complied with Hannah's wishes and scurried toward the other room. It was easy to comply, as they knew the door to the kitchen was thin and they could plant their ears firmly against the wood to hear the entire conversation. They didn't want to miss a thing.

"Stick, sit down." Hannah seemed too calm. Stick was almost breathless with fear of what she was going to say.

After he settled down on the couch, Hannah looked him square in the eyes and proceeded to speak.

"Stick, you know that I love you. You don't doubt that for one minute, I'm sure."

"And I love you too, Hannah, please let me..."

"Don't interrupt me, Stick. I've had eleven hours to think about all of this and I want to say what I want to say straight out to you. I'm not holding anything back."

Stick could feel the sweat trickling down his face.

"We got married for all of the right reasons. We love each other, and we want to spend the rest of our lives together. We also have told ourselves, from the get go, that a lot changed after your accident, and we would face some bad times. With that being said, I believe we are probably both in denial about how bad those bad times can be. We've been going through the motions with our heads in the sand, Stick. We are being naïve thinking that you, living with pain, is not going to be a mountain of an issue in our lives. We are going to need help with this. Lots of help. I don't know from where yet, but we are for sure going to need help from God to show us what to do." Hannah lowered her head to gather her thoughts for the rest of her heart-to-heart with her husband.

Stick never for once doubted her determination. Her jaw was set, and he knew she meant every word coming from her mouth.

"Now, Stick, I'm going to say this once and once only. I'm in this for the long haul with you under one condition. There's one condition that is a deal breaker. Are you listening to me, Stick? I want to make sure that you are hearing everything that I say because I'm only going to say this one time."

"I am. I am." Stick looked at Hannah with a steady stream of tears rolling down his cheeks.

"No more alcohol. Ever. Do you hear me? If you choose alcohol, you choose it alone."

"I hear you, Hannah. Loud and clear. Nothing is more important to me in my life than you. I never want to lose you."

"Good, Stick. You better mean that because losing me would also mean that you would lose our child."

Hannah's mother and Marlene Frye almost fell through the swinging door. A baby? Did Hannah just tell Stick that she was going to have a baby?

Stick jumped up from the couch and went over to Hannah. He gently took her hands in his, pulled her up and into his arms. They both wept quietly as their embrace said everything that needed to be said.

Except for one thing.

"Oh, and Stick, I know that you have no feeling in your right butt cheek and you didn't know that Barbie had a firm grip on it last night."

Barbie had gripped his butt cheek? Stick was mortified. He vowed, then and there, with his head hung low, that he would spend the rest of his life making Hannah happy. He was going to be a daddy and he would prove to Hannah that she had made the right choice to marry him. He could fix all of this. He was determined and had no fear that he couldn't live up to his promises. He just prayed under his breath that Hannah had not told his mom about Barbie and his butt cheek.

CHAPTER 30:

A Small Frye Is Born

Milton Edward Frye was born in Miami Baptist Hospital on a sweltering summer day in August of 1972. All relatives of Stick and Hannah Frye that proudly stood peeking through the hospital nursery window, declared without hesitation that he was the cutest and most perfect child that had ever been born, Jesus aside.

A baby made them a family of three, and according to God's plan, Stick and Hannah had recently been approved for a loan to purchase a small farm on the outskirts of Blackjack Hollow, Oklahoma. Hannah's parents and Marlene Frye had generously helped them with a down payment and their dream to own a farm was coming to fruition.

Most profoundly, Stick had stood by his word and had not touched a drop of alcohol since that day in the Kimball's living room in Madill, Oklahoma. He had found a new doctor in Tulsa that had gotten his pain somewhat under control. Blackjack Hollow was a short drive into the city, but remote enough to live the country lifestyle that he and Hannah had always wanted.

Stick had come to grips with the fact that the pain would never go away completely. A strong faith in God, a beautiful and loving wife, and now a son to raise, kept it all in prospective for Stick Frye. However, there was something else that kept him focused. He wanted to make his dad proud too. Besides the apparition in the operating room that changed his life forever, Stick had only one other memory of the first days in the hospital after his accident and he would never forget that memory as long as he lived. Stick Frye remembered his dad running alongside the gurney, holding his son's hand as he kept saying, "I will never leave you, son."

Stick always felt like his dad was nearby and he sensed his presence most strongly when he needed to talk to someone. Boots was always there exactly when he needed him. Boots Frye would enter Stick's mind with a peace. It was nothing spectacular, just a gentle peace, often followed by memories of sage offerings of advice that Boots had left behind. Always spot on.

He wanted to make his dad proud.

CHAPTER 31

Nailin' Down His Name

Stick Frye loved being a daddy. He insisted on taking his baby son on a walk around the farm first thing every morning since the day he and Hannah moved to Blackjack Hollow. Stick was proud to see how his son was excited to be around the animals on the farm. His little son was not afraid to hang out with the cows, pigs, and chickens and Stick loved hearing him try to moo, oink and cluck. Just like the animals in their barnyard.

He was also proud to have named his son Milton. Stick had been named Milton after Boot's father, Milton, and Edward, after Boot's himself and Hannah was in complete agreement that carrying on the family name was a good thing to do.

Truthfully, they were also in agreement that as soon as they could nail down little Milton's personality, a suitable nickname was a must. Milton looked good on a birth certificate but that was about it.

"Hey, Hannah. Did you ever see the Disney movie from the '60's, Swiss Family Robinson? It was my favorite movie to watch with my dad. We always talked about someday building a big treehouse kinda like the one they lived in."

"I did see that movie, Stick. I loved it too!"

"Well, I was thinkin' the other day about my favorite character in that movie. It was the mischievous one with freckles, Moochie. Do you remember him? He was so funny."

Hannah laughed and said she did remember Moochie.

"Little Milton reminds me of him a lot. Does he you?" Stick was bouncing his baby son on his knee.

"He really does, Stick. Are you thinking about calling him Moochie?" Hannah grimaced at the thought of her child being referred to as a Moochie. Like a mooch. She could imagine the teasing that would surely happen.

"Actually, Hannah, I kinda like the name Mookie. I don't know why, but I think it just fits him. What do you think?"

They both watched their baby bounce up and down on Stick's knee. He was smiling and wrinkling up his little button of a nose.

"I like it, Stick! I think he is a Mookie. Mookie Frye. Yes, let's call him Mookie."

Milton Edward Frye, became Mookie Frye and it fit him to a T.

CHAPTER 32:

The Pathway Is Forged

Stick was a natural at being a farmer. He tackled farming with the same fervor as he had tackled sports. One of his idols was Vince Lombardi and he tried to emulate Vince's "winners never quit, and quitters never win" attitude. However, some days were better than others, and after a particularly troublesome day on the farm, a frustrated Stick walked over to his work bench in the barn and turned on his Panasonic AM FM radio. It was noon and he knew the cattle market report was being broadcasted by the local radio station. Stick would be taking a trailer load of fall calves to the stockyard the following week for the weekly cattle auction and the paycheck for the sale could make or break his and Hannah's bank account for the remainder of the year.

The young couple tried their best to live as frugally as they could, and it was evident to them both that there were no more corners to cut. The turnip could be squeezed tighter and tighter but not a drop of blood would come forth. Those calves needed to bring top dollar going into winter or the Fryes would be in a painful financial bind.

Farming could be rewarding or crushing. It all hinged on the market. Stick and Hannah's livelihood was at the mercy of the "powers that be" that drove the cattle prices up or down. So many factors were out of the lowly farmers' control. Corn prices, wheat prices, weather, fuel, the state of the Union, and behind the scenes manipulations. There was nothing the farmers could do but keep doing what they knew worked to send healthy, and well-fed cattle to the sale barns. They would roll the dice each calving season, and after the animals were delivered to the stockyard to be sold, they would pray the paycheck that arrived had enough numbers on it to get them through until it all started over again.

Stick stood in front of his work bench waiting for the commercial to come to an end, as the evocative sounding girl in the Noxzema medicated shave cream commercial murmured "take it off, take it all off" before the ag reporter began to tick off the average market prices for beef.

"Thank you, Sweet Jesus!" Cattle prices were up by a nice, steady margin and Stick was relieved. Even though he was happy with the news of the day in the world of agriculture, he felt like he needed a daily reminder to keep all things farming in prospective. Stick grabbed the number two pencil he had stuck behind his ear, licked the graphite that he had whittled to a nice, sharp point, and proceeded to scribble a quote from Dwight D. Eisenhower. He wrote it lengthwise on a sheet of paper he had torn from a Big Chief tablet. "You know, farming looks mighty easy when your plow is a pencil, and you're a thousand miles from the corn field." Two thumb tacks on the upper corners later and his frustration was visible to all as he took his hammer and tapped the tacks into place above his work bench.

Stick took a lot of pride in his pasture management skills, and his growing herd of sleek, fatted, Black Angus cattle. He began every day by driving around in his old farm truck checking every head of cattle to make sure all the herd was accounted for and there were no signs of illness among the animals. Therefore, after listening to the cattle report, and feeling satisfied that he had put in a full morning of farming chores, Stick decided to turn the tuning knob on his radio to listen to Denny Matthews, broadcasting out of Kansas City, Missouri. Denny Matthews had been the broadcasting voice for the Kansas City Royals since their inception in 1969. In northeastern Oklahoma, there were two major league baseball teams that most of the folks followed with passion and devotion. The New York Yankees, obviously due to the fame of the Oklahoma native son, Mickey Mantle, and the St. Louis Cardinals, simply because Missouri was in the same neck-of-the-woods as Oklahoma. The fans were diehards. Decades of devotion, with many hours of sitting underneath nearby shade trees, with a cold piece of watermelon, a frosty lemonade or refreshing sweet tea, and an old radio tuned in to the lazy Saturday afternoon baseball games. "Take Me Out to the Ballgame" loudly and blusteringly sang by Chicago Cubs announcer, Harry Caray at the seventh inning stretch, and the Gillette shaving commercials "to look good and feel good too, Gillette is the one for you", echoing from one backyard to the next. Stick had been a devotee of the New York Yankees in his teen years but was now a rabid fan of the newer team hailing from Kansas City. The Kansas City Royals had won Stick over when they quickly became a powerhouse in the American League. It was 1976, and Stick Frye was rooting his team on to win the division. His favorite player was third baseman, and designated hitter, George Brett. A poster of George hung in Stick's barn. Every morning, before he headed out to do his chores, Stick Frye stood in front of the glossy poster on the weathered barn wall. George Brett had achieved the dream of being in the big leagues that Stick Frye could never again hope to accomplish. He wasn't a bit bitter about it though. He was happy for George. A true sport doesn't get jealous of others. A true sport loves the game so much that he recognizes all the hard work it takes to get to the top. Stick Frye enjoyed standing in front of the famous third baseman's poster every morning. Every kid deserves a chance to reach the pinnacle if he has the talent and fortitude. George Brett got that chance and made it. Stick Frye had a son. Maybe someday his son would like to have the chance to make it too.

Stick had a feeling about Mookie. Mookie Frye, four years old, was already showing a natural talent of an athlete. There was something special about his kid. If the truth was known, Boots Frye probably saw the same thing in Stick when he was little. If George Brett could do it, so could Mookie. Stick was determined to help forge a pathway for Mookie if his boy had the desire. Whatever it took.

That was the baseball side of Stick. On the other hand, George Brett wasn't the only face that got a tip of the cowboy hat each morning in Stick Frye's barn. In a corner of the barn hung an old rodeo poster. Jim Shoulders had brought it to him when he was in the hospital after the accident. It was the day of his father's funeral, and even though he had good company with Hannah sitting with him, he didn't feel like talking, or eating, or even breathing. Heck, he didn't feel much like living himself that day. Lying on the hospital bed, confined by the body cast, and missing his father, Stick was depressed beyond measure that he was unable to be in Tishomingo with his family to say one last farewell to Boots Frye. The best dad on earth.

Even though he had his eyes closed, Stick could tell that someone had entered his hospital room. As he opened his eyes to a slight squint, he couldn't believe what he saw. Standing there in person, in real life, was the great Jim Shoulders. His idol in the world of rodeo.

He was definitely star struck but had a great conversation with the old rodeo cowboy. Stick was so grateful when Jim Shoulders pulled the rolled-up poster out of his jacket pocket, placed it on Stick's hospital bed tray, took out his ink pen, and wrote across the bottom of the poster. "To the best rodeo champ that ever came out of a chute. Stick Frye – 8 seconds on El Diablo." He then scribbled his autograph underneath and handed the poster to the eighteen-year-old, beat up, busted up, and grinning, Stick Frye.

Stick loved that old poster and everything that it represented. He would often run his hand over its slick surface, conjuring up memories of bull rides of his own past. The picture of Jim Shoulders atop an angry, and snorting bull brought chills up and down his spine. He could almost hear the crowd whoopin' and hollerin' and could imagine the sound of the buzzer. The signal that the ride was over sometimes came before the eight-second mark for some bull riders, but Stick Frye most usually held on for dear life and enjoyed the ride until the full eight seconds were spent. He knew he would never forget those memories as long as he lived.

Furthermore, the undeniable fact was that Stick had never lost his love for the thrill that was the game of baseball and he couldn't contain his desire to be in the stands when the gates flew open and a pawing, shimmying, and muscled-up bull came out of the chute like a freight train. The two sports were indelibly stamped on his heart and soul, and the truth of the matter, he realized he would forever be a spectator. He had come to grips with that, the hand that he was dealt. Just like his dad, Boots, you take the hand you get dealt.

That was something he pondered almost every day of his life. The hands that people get dealt. The control, or lack thereof. Futures. His and Hannah's future and especially the future of his pride and joy, his tow-headed son, Mookie. He couldn't help but worry a bit about Mookie. Stick Frye was most definitely a ponderer, not a lamenter, mind you, just a ponderer, and he often found himself thinking about Mookie's future. He wanted Mookie to have dreams and to be able to follow his dreams.

He vowed to never rain on Mookie's parade with a sad attitude about how his own dreams were halted on that Saturday night those years ago. Everything about how Stick loved baseball and rodeo was going to be kept positive. Fact of the matter, Stick Frye wanted to instill in his son the same love for the two sports that he had. There was nothing wrong in taking his boy to as many games and rodeos as he could. Hannah would love it too. He just knew it.

"Daddy, the man on the radio just said George Brett hit a home run!"

"He did? Come here, buddy, let's sit here and listen together."

The path was being forged.

CHAPTER 33

A Popular Kid, that Mookie Frye

The Frye family settled in quite nicely into the community of Blackjack Hollow, Oklahoma. Hannah made fast friends with other farm wives, Stick carried on many over-the-fence "solving-the-world's-problems" conversations with his neighboring farmers, and little Mookie was the most popular kid in his third-grade class. Why was he the most popular kid? Mookie Frye was solid and genuine, sweet, and kind, and all the other traits that make a likeable kid popular. Was that why? Sure, it was. But along with being a neat kid, there was a big bonus being friends with Mookie. An undeniably big bonus if you are a third-grade boy in Blackjack Hollow, Oklahoma.

What was the bonus? Mookie Frye believed in Bigfoot. What third-grader didn't want to hang around a kid that believed in Bigfoot?

Mookie was "all in" with being a true believer in the cryptid, the simian-like creature of American folklore that is said to inhabit forests in

North America. Big, hairy, mysterious creatures with lots of bizarre and inexplicable folklore surrounding the debate of whether they truly exist or are the product of a big hoax.

So, what hooked Mookie Frye?

The summer before Mookie went into third-grade, he and his dad, Stick, were picking up bags of creep feed for the calves at the local feed store when they heard a commotion outside on Main Street. Stick, Mookie, and the other patrons of the store, dropped what they were doing and scurried out the door to see what was happening. The first thing Stick and Mookie noticed was a news truck from KTUL TV in Tulsa, parked in front of the police station. There was a crowd of about twenty people standing around the truck as the reporter and his cameraman, camera rolling, were in the process of doing a live, televised interview with Buddy Tempey, the Blackjack Hollow police chief.

"Chief Tempey, do you have any information regarding what is being called a Bigfoot sighting in your area?" the inquisitive reporter pushed his microphone toward Chief Tempey's face.

"Well, boys, word of this so-called sighting," Chief Tempey looked toward the crowd and with a big wink and a chuckle, continued, "yes, word of this so-called sighting just reached me a few minutes ago and I haven't had enough time to send one of my deputies out to investigate. Honestly, I'm surprised that you have jumped on this with such fervor. Must be a slow news day in Tulsa." Chief Tempey winked again and the crowd let out hearty laughs.

"Actually, Chief Tempey, we have information from a reliable source that there is some kind of physical evidence. A bone, perhaps, or some hair, maybe? Have you heard anything about physical evidence?"

"Who is your reliable source? Could it be Edwinna Blackworth?" Chief Tempey shot a huge smile at the crowd, which they answered with a new round of belly laughs.

"Why, yes, Edwinna Blackworth is our source. She described herself as the city librarian and historian. Are these not her correct credentials?" The reporter again thrust the microphone toward Chief Tempey.

"Not to disparage the reputation of the lovely Miss Blackworth, or to trivialize her standing in this community, but, gentlemen, Edwinna Blackworth is a kook! You can quote me on that. Now if you will excuse me, I have much bigger fish to fry than to stand around here jacking my jaw with you fellows over something as ridiculous as a made-up Bigfoot sighting. Jiminy Christmas! Have a good day." Chief Tempey gently pushed the microphone back toward the reporter, stepped off the curb, and strolled nonchalantly toward the Kozy Kitchen Diner. Thick, black coffee, crispy bacon, eggs over medium, and homemade cinnamon rolls were calling his name and he'd be darned if he was going to waste his time over another hair-brained, trumped-up bit of nonsense perpetrated by that goose, Edwinna Blackstock. Didn't she have anything better to do?

As all eyes were on the exiting police chief's back, the television reporter turned toward the crowd of people and asked them if anyone could give them directions to Charley Bowman's farm. A voice in the group began ticking off the route to Charley Bowman's place while the cameraman used an ink pen to scribble each turn, mile-marker, and landmark down on the palm of his hand. Satisfied that they could maneuver the trip, the two men jumped back into the news truck and proceeded to pull out of the parking place.

"Come on, Mookie. Let's go check this out!" Stick and Mookie jumped into their truck and got in line, as did several of the other spectators. It was a caravan of curiosity seekers heading to the outskirts of town, straight to the residence of Charley Bowman, local farmer, and Commander of the Blackjack Hollow chapter of the VFW.

Charley Bowman had a reputation of being a straight shooter. A man's man.

"I have a feeling this is gonna get good, Mookie." Stick winked at his son, and Mookie smiled back. Mookie could hardly contain his excitement as they followed close behind the news truck. Straight toward Charley Bowman's farm.

CHAPTER 34

Big-Eyed Charley Bowman

When they pulled into Charley Bowman's front yard, the newsmen were already knocking on his front door. Stick put his truck into park just as Charley Bowman opened his door to see the reporters in his doorway and a passel of local townspeople converging on his front lawn.

Charley sauntered out onto his porch, took a look around at the gathering crowd, and proceeded to pull a bandana from his back pocket. As he wiped the back of his neck with the bandana, the reporter and cameraman pulled their microphone and camera out of the bag, turned on the switches, and began to speak to Charley Bowman.

"Mr. Bowman, we are with KTUL TV in Tulsa and we are here to ask you some questions about a possible Bigfoot sighting here on your property last night. Would you mind giving us a few moments of your time?"

Charley stuffed the bandana back into his pocket, looked around at the crowd, and as he began to speak, his eyes got bigger than silver dollars. Stick Frye whispered to his son Mookie that he had never seen that look on Charley Bowman's face before, not even when he won the raffle prize of a new truck last Christmas. Nope, Stick had never seen Charley Bowman's eyes ever get that big.

"Well, fellers, I don't even know where to start. You'll have to bear with me 'cause I didn't get a wink of sleep last night. Couldn't sleep a wink after all the commotion, that's for sure."

"Sir, can you tell us, the best way you can, what happened here last night?"

"I reckon I can. To start, I guess I will have you look over yonder at my chicken coop. Do you see where the door to the coop has been pulled off its hinges? Trashed my chicken coop door, for sure, that varmint. Took off with two of my best layers. Made me madder than a hornet in an old beer can. By the time I ran in to get my shotgun, he was gone. I fired at him but missed. He had already gotten outta range."

"Can you start at the beginning, Mr. Bowman? How did you know there was something going on out here? Did you get a good look at him? The varmint. Did you see what was taking your chickens?" The news reporter was peppering Charley Bowman with questions.

Charley didn't skip a beat as he reeled off the previous night's adventure to the crowd.

"I'm usually a light sleeper, but my wife heard it before I did. She was elbowin' me pretty good and when I got my wits about me it was a full-on uproar. We jumped outta bed and I ran out there. I still can't believe I didn't grab my gun on the way out. That's not like me at all. But anyway, I hurried out to the porch, and was tryin' to get my boots on when I saw him. My wife, Annie, flipped on the porch light at that same time and there he was. Bigger than Dallas. Tall as me. Hair all over his body. Standin' out there in the chicken coop, holdin' my two best layin' hens. And then he just took off runnin'. Fast too. I stepped into my house, grabbed my 410, aimed and fired right at him. I can tell you he never looked back. Just ran up that hill into those woods over there. Tore my door off, took my chickens and ran off. Never seen anything like it in all my life."

There was a deafening silence from the onlookers and the television reporter was at a total loss for words. The camera kept right on rolling, panning the faces, and capturing the individual expressions of the stunned crowd. Right there in Charley Bowman's front yard.

The reporter's head dropped down for a moment while he regained his thoughts, then he motioned to the cameraman to turn the camera on him. He stared pensively into the lens and spoke directly to the television audience, whoever they were out there in the TV land. "Well, folks, there you have it. Digest it however you choose. Believe or not. Jack Lively, signing off here in Blackjack Hollow, Oklahoma."

The television crew calmly packed up their camera and microphone, loaded up the news truck, took one last glance around the farm, turned the key in the ignition, slowly backed out of Charley Bowman's front yard, and drove off. Back to Tulsa, to the world of reality. No Bigfoot sightings in Tulsa, and for what it's worth, no Tooth Fairy or Santa Claus sightings there either.

Due to the total silence in the vehicle as it headed back to Tulsa, it was a given that a stop at Arnie's Bar was next on their agenda. As soon as they hit Tulsa, they would have to have a drink. Perhaps even several.

The two news staffers never mentioned Charley Bowman, the yanked off door to the chicken coop, or the bizarre tale of the hairy creature, to each other again. They feared they would become absolute laughingstocks in their industry. Individually though, that was a different story. Many nights after that, when their houses were still and quiet, their heads were sunk down in the coolness of their pillows, and the moon was shining through their windows, they would wonder. They both had stood right there on Charley Bowman's front porch and heard the story. Straight from Charley Bowman's lips. There was no doubt in either of their minds that Charley Bowman had no agenda at all in the telling of the turn of events of that night. Heck, he hadn't even been the one to report it to the news. Edwinna Blackworth, the librarian and historian, had stopped by Annie Bowman's house that next morning after the episode to bring a book by to her friend, Annie. That's when Edwinna heard Charley and Annie's account of Bigfoot and the chicken coop incident. She is the one that called the news desk as soon as she arrived at her job at the Blackjack Hollow Public Library. Charley and Annie had no clue that Edwinna was going to call the news. When Edwinna dialed the television station, she is the one that sounded credible to the news desk clerk. The television news desk clerk had heard it all over the years and she was very adept at call screening. Edwinna had convinced her. Despite that, the news guys had each heard Chief Tempey label Edwinna as a kook and that unabashed description weighed heavily on their minds. Nonetheless, Charley Bowman was a different story. They believed him. They both believed Charley Bowman.

So did Mookie Frye.

As they stood in Charley Bowman's front yard on that fateful day, Stick and Mookie knew that ol' Charley's life would never be the same

THE SETTING SON

going forward. Soon after the news truck pulled out onto the highway, the jibs, jabs and jokes came flooding forth.

"Hey, Charley, is your hairy friend gonna come back tonight for chicken and dumplins'?"

"I guess Bigfoot is supplying the chicken, huh?"

"Hey, Charley, are you sure that wasn't your daughter's new boyfriend sneakin' around your chicken coop last night? I heard he was kinda hairy!"

Knee slapping, and belly laughs from everyone. Everyone except Stick and Mookie, that is.

Stick couldn't hold back any longer. "Hey, y'all. Leave Charley alone, why don't ya? The man simply told us what he saw. Give him a break. Get on outta here and just leave him be if you can't be decent."

A confused Charley Bowman stood on his front porch with his arms crossed across his chest. These people were supposed to be his friends and neighbors. All of them. He was being ridiculed and poked fun of by the same men that stood next to him each Sunday where they served as ushers in the local Baptist church. The same men that attended meetings at the VFW with him. The same men that hadn't hesitated to call him when they needed his help with a distressed cow with a breech calf hung up in the birth canal and Charley never thought twice about dropping whatever it was he was doing to go help a fellow farmer in need. Strong Charley Bowman could reach in a momma cow and pull a calf out in a split second. Many farmers in those parts had called on Charley when they needed help with their cows. His neighbors were standing there in his yard poking fun of him and he was befuddled and mortified.

Time didn't soften their sentiments, and sadly to say for Charley, the townspeople never let up on him. Charley Bowman became the laughingstock of Blackjack Hollow, Oklahoma. He endured relentless teasing and taunting over the years from the folks he had previously counted as friends and neighbors, which caused him to become more and more withdrawn from the community. On the rare occasion that found him in town to purchase supplies, Charley presented himself as someone with thick enough skin to handle their mocking and would readily tell them all to go fly a kite, but deep inside it was very difficult for him.

The madder Charley got at his neighbors, the more sympathy he had for Bigfoot. The truth is, Charley Bowman had a strong sense that Bigfoot was out there. Out there over the horizon watching and thinking. He felt his presence. Charley's gut told him that Bigfoot lurked in the distance, just far enough away to be hidden from the eye of the world, but close enough to keep a keen eye on his surroundings. Bigfoot was watching the woods, watching the town, and watching the people.

Charley reasoned with himself that Bigfoot was hungry the night he tore the door off the chicken coop. The creature probably didn't mean any harm, he was just hungry. Therefore, Charley hid an aluminum wash pan out by an old stump just inside the wooded area to the north of his barn. Every Friday night, Charley would fill the pan with some grilled hamburger patties, several hot dogs, and a generous piece of Annie's famous coconut cream pie. Charley would check the pan the next morning and all the food would be gone. He wondered at first if it was just an old stray dog that had happened upon it or some other kind of varmints that helped themselves to the food in the wash pan. Eventually, however, his curiosity got the better of him. Therefore, late one Friday night, Charley decided to crawl out of bed, put his clothes on, and sneak out by the woods to see if he could catch a glimpse of who, or what, was eating the food.

In his astonishment, as soon as he crouched down to take a peek, there he was.

Bigfoot was sitting on the stump, with his silhouette outlined by the glow of the moon. The shiny aluminum wash pan was nestled in his lap, he was slowly and methodically picking up the food with his hand, raising it to his lips, and taking small bites.

The hair stood out on Charley's neck as he watched the creature gaze up at the moon, continuing to take meager tastes of the food from the wash pan. The creature seemed deep in thought and Charley Bowman whispered to himself that he would give anything to know what was going through the hairy guy's mind.

As he hid behind the old oak tree, frozen like a statue and staring at the shaggy animal, his jaw suddenly dropped all the way down to his chin. Bigfoot placed a piece of food in his mouth and deliberately turned his head toward Charley Bowman. He peered directly at Charley's face, continuing to slowly chew the food. Their eyes made contact, and at that brief moment in time, Charley was convinced he saw into Bigfoot's heart and soul. Goosebumps covered Charley's body as he pondered to himself, "Was Bigfoot more human than animal?"

After a moment, Bigfoot turned his head back around and directed his eyes toward the moon seeming to be deep in thought. With Charley Bowman crouched motionless in his spot at the edge of the forest, the hairy creature stood up, placed the wash pan behind him on the stump, and quickly stole away into the night.

Charley Bowman swore, then and there, that he would never tell a soul about Bigfoot. Not even Annie.

CHAPTER 35

Bigfoot and the Visitors

On the way back to the feed store, Stick asked Mookie what he thought about the happenings they just witnessed in Charley Bowman's front yard.

"Why were those people laughing at Charley, dad? They were being mean, weren't they?"

"Hmmm. Well, son, I think they were teasin' him and yeah, they did kinda go overboard with it. Probably took it too far."

"Dad, I believe Charley. Don't you? Do you believe Charley?"

"You know, Mookie, I've known Charley Bowman for several years now and I've never taken him for some kind of weirdo. He's always been a straight shooter as far as I know. If I had to decide right here and now, I'm on the side of believin' that Charley described exactly what he believed he saw last night. Was it Bigfoot? I don't have a clue. Have I ever seen a creature that stands up tall as Charley Bowman and has hair all over his body? No. Can't say that I ever have. I saw Charley's face when he was givin' his account of what he saw, just the same as you, Mookie, and Charley did not make that part up. I suppose I'm with you, Mookie. I guess I believe Charley Bowman."

Charley appreciated how Stick and Mookie stood up for him that morning on his porch. They were the only ones that continued to treat him with respect and he knew he could trust them. That's exactly why he was dialing Stick Frye's home phone number that morning, two weeks after the incident.

"Frye residence. Mookie Frye speaking." Hannah made sure that her son had good manners and was polite when answering the telephone.

"Good morning, Mookie. Can I please speak to your father? This is Charley Bowman callin'." Mookie said hello to Charley, then ran to the barn to fetch his dad.

"Dad! Dad! Telephone! It's Charley Bowman." Stick Frye stuck his head out of the barn door, wiping his hands on an old rag, and hollered to Mookie to tell Charley that he would be right there.

"Mornin', Charley. What can I do for ya?"

"Howdy, Stick. I hope I didn't take you away from anything important, but I wanted to call and see if you and Mookie might want to come over to my place and take a look at what's goin' on over here."

"Why sure, Charley. We'll head on over right now."

"Alrighty then. And, hey, if you don't mind, could ya not tell anyone that you're comin' over? I'd kinda like to keep this thing under wraps."

Stick assured Charley Bowman that he would stay mum and he and Mookie piled into the truck to head Charley's way. Mookie just knew it had something to do with Bigfoot.

Mookie hadn't stopped thinking about Bigfoot for the whole two weeks since they went to Charley Bowman's place. He had begged his mom to take him to the library the very next day, so he could check out as many books as he could about Bigfoot, Sasquatch, or Yetis. Lucky for him, the head librarian was the one to stamp the due dates on the card in the sleeve that was glued on the inside cover of each book.

"You've picked out some very interesting reading material, Mookie. Are you doing a school project about Bigfoot?" Edwinna Blackworth, head librarian and historian, peered over her half glasses at the youngster as Mookie waited patiently for his books. The maximum allowed to check out was six. He had placed seven books on the counter.

"No, ma'am. There's no school project. I just wanted to learn as much as I can about it. It's like a hobby, I guess." Mookie kept his eye on Edwinna's date stamper. As she and Mookie talked, she got closer and closer to the seventh book.

"We just got a couple of these books in last week. I haven't had a chance to look at them yet. Very interesting subject." She seemed deep in thought as the date stamper embossed the required return date on one book after the other. Their eyes met as she came to the seventh book.

"The limit is six books, Mookie. I see here that you have seven. Is there one that you would like to put back to check out later?"

As Edwinna Blackworth looked up from her date stamping, she saw the pained expression on Mookie's face. Smiling inwardly, she thought to herself that she once knew a little girl that went full speed ahead, no holds barred, when something exciting peaked her interest. Actually, maybe that little girl still existed. Perhaps she had just gotten a little bit older.

"I tell you what, Mookie. I will go ahead and let you take all seven books today if you will promise me something."

"Yes, ma'am. What is it?" A relieved Mookie Frye looked back at Edwinna Blackworth with his bright and shining blue eyes.

"When you get all your research done, how about I invite you and your parents to my house for dinner and we can discuss what you've learned? How would that be?"

"I think it sounds great, Miss Blackworth. I will have to talk to my parents about it, but I'm sure they will say yes." Mookie smiled even bigger when Edwinna Blackworth pushed down on her date stamper with an audible click, and the seventh book was checked out in his name. All seven books were legitimately checked out. Mookie was beaming.

Edwinna helped Mookie get the library books neatly placed into his canvas bag.

"Enjoy your reading, Mookie." Edwinna came around from the counter and gently patted Mookie Frye on the back as she helped him place his book bag strap on his shoulder. As he started to walk away, she leaned down and whispered into Mookie's ear.

"I believe Charley Bowman too, Mookie."

Mookie rushed home with his books and dug right in. He had all seven books read by the end of the two weeks since the incident.

Mookie could barely contain his excitement as he and his dad drove out to Charley Bowman's on that crisp October morning.

There was a beat-up old red Jeep Wagoneer parked in front of Charley Bowman's house when Stick and Mookie pulled into the lane that led directly to the Bowman's farmhouse. Stick noticed that it carried a license plate on it from Colorado. Two young men in their early twenties were sitting on Annie and Charley Bowman's front porch. Annie Bowman had fixed a fresh pot of coffee and a plate of fruit-filled fried pies, dusted with powdered sugar, graced the wooden table in front of the porch swing.

Charley Bowman came out of the front door and stood on the first step of the porch as Stick and Mookie opened the doors to the truck and started walking toward the house.

"Dusty and Henry, this is a good friend and neighbor, Stick Frye and his son, Mookie." The two Coloradoans rose from their chairs and thrust their hands toward Stick and Mookie.

"Stick, Mookie, these fellers are Dusty and Henry Waters from somewhere in Colorado. Where did you two say you lived?" Charley turned back toward Dusty after the initial introductions.

"Yes, Mr. Bowman, let me introduce us. Stick, Mookie, my name is Dusty Waters, and this is my brother, Henry Waters. We live in Niwot, Colorado. Just outside of Boulder. You've heard of Boulder, haven't you, Mr. Frye?"

"Please just call me Stick. Yes, I do know where Boulder is. My dad and mom and I drove through there on our way up to Sterling for a junior rodeo championship when I was in the seventh grade."

After the introductions, the men settled in with cups of strong coffee, and Annie fixed Mookie a cup of hot chocolate, to go along with their fried pies.

"As I was telling Mr. Bowman," Dusty decided to get the conversation brought to the subject at hand, "my brother and I are here to see if we could get Charley's permission to allow us to check out his property. We heard about the possible Bigfoot sighting, and we are amateur Bigfoot detectives. We've done some other sighting documentations, but never one in Oklahoma."

"Amateur Bigfoot detectives?" Mookie Frye had never heard anything more exciting in his life.

Charley told Dusty and Henry that they could investigate all they wanted, as long as they didn't bother his cows. They assured him that their tactics were simple and non-intrusive, and they got right to work.

Charley had chores to do but told Stick and Mookie they were welcomed to hang out and watch the detectives do their thing. Stick and Mookie thought watching the two detectives at work sounded a whole lot better than painting fence posts back at the Frye farm, so they thanked Charley for the invitation and proceeded to follow close behind and see what Dusty and Henry Waters' plan of action was going to entail.

"Hey, Dusty, can you go out to the Jeep and get the bag of plaster of Paris? I'll get some water in the bucket." Henry Waters stood at the edge of the Bowman's front porch with the plastic bucket and stir stick. Charley Bowman had shown them where to find the water spigot on the side of the house.

Mookie whispered to his dad, "Hey, dad, what is plaster of Paris?"

"I'll be danged if I know, son. I guess we'll just have to watch and see." Stick and Mookie followed Henry to the side of the house, as he turned the water on to fill the one-gallon plastic bucket.

As Dusty sifted the white powdery substance into the bucket filled with water, Henry used the stir stick to make sure it was kept at a smooth consistency of pancake batter.

"Okay, let's head over to the chicken coop. We need to hurry and get some footprint casts before this stuff sets up."

Footprints? What the heck were they talking about? Mookie Frye was so intrigued.

Dusty and Henry wandered around the yard in the chicken coop area.

"Here's a couple of great ones. I can see the whole foot!"

Dusty knelt down and ever so lightly brushed away bits of leaves and sticks from the footprint, taking care not to disturb the footprint itself. Henry carefully poured the plaster of Paris mixture around the edge, letting it seep down into the footprint.

"We do it this way, so the mixture doesn't mess up any of the footprint. It works better if it slowly seeps into the print instead of going directly down into it."

Mookie watched closely, not wanting to miss anything.

After they had poured the mixture into six footprints, Henry told Mookie and Stick they would need to let the plaster casts sit and harden for about an hour before they could pop them out of the ground. They all decided to walk around the perimeter of the Bowman's yard to see if they could see any other signs of Bigfoot while they waited for the casts to dry.

Mookie was making mental notes of everything the Waters brothers were doing. Being a Bigfoot detective seemed like something that every third-grade boy would want to do. He didn't want to miss a thing.

Dusty Waters took several pictures with their Polaroid. Mookie and Stick watched as the prints appeared instantly on the photo paper. Henry and Dusty explained that they would take the pictures back to Colorado with them where they could spend some time taking a closer look at the photographs of the perimeter of Charley's yard for possible answers to their questions about the Bigfoot sighting.

"Mookie, we can see that you have a keen interest in our investigative work. Dusty and I have decided to give you a set of the plaster of Paris footprints that we made here in the chicken coop. We feel like we have enough good ones to do what we need to do when we get back to Colorado." Henry Waters handed over the pair of footprints to Mookie. They had carefully wrapped them in newspaper and secured the paper with masking tape. "Handle them carefully, and here's our address and phone number. Don't hesitate to call us if you have any questions."

Mookie had never been more thrilled in his life as when Henry and Dusty Waters handed over the set of footprints to him.

Mookie took a mental note of the type of camera that Henry and Dusty used. It had Polaroid 350 written on its side. It looked pretty old and Mookie didn't remember ever seeing one like it. Maybe his mom, Hannah, could help him find one. The list was growing. Plaster of Paris, buckets, water, and an instamatic camera.

"Can I be a Bigfoot detective, dad?" Stick only had one leg up in the truck before Mookie blurted out his question.

They had just said goodbye to Henry and Dusty Waters and waved at Charley Bowman out on his tractor in his hay meadow. Stick looked over at his son, Mookie, with a grin.

"I don't see why not."

Mookie couldn't wait to tell his mom.

CHAPTER 36:

The Perplexities of Butch Ed Baxter

Mookie Frye had two best friends. Stoney Allen had been his first best friend since kindergarten. Stoney's dad, Satch, was the Blackjack Hollow High School principal. Stoney had a cute, and goofy younger sister, Forrestette (they called her "Frosty" for short.) Mookie loved to tease Frosty and she didn't seem to mind it too awful much.

Mookie's second-best friend moved in to the farm next door to the Frye's farm the summer before his second grade. His name was Butch Ed Baxter. Mookie, Stoney, and Butch Ed became fast and inseparable friends.

Stick and Hannah Frye were the first to welcome the Baxter family to their neck-of-the woods.

"Stick, I baked a pineapple upside down cake to take over to the new neighbors. I thought maybe after supper we could go over there and say hello." Stick thought that sounded like a very nice gesture, and as soon as they had eaten, Stick, Hannah, and Mookie, piled into their truck and headed south to the neighboring farm, pineapple upside down cake in tow.

It seemed to take an extra bit of time for the Baxters to open their front door after Stick tapped lightly on the wooden frame of the screen door. They could hear muffled voices inside the home as they stood conspicuously on the front porch, like stair steps. Stick, Hannah, Mookie, and the cake. Their awkward smiles were about to wane when the door flew open and a mirror-like stair step family stood facing the Fryes.

"Hello! Who do we have here? Please come right in." Mr. Baxter, held the front door open for the cake-bearing guests. Mrs. Baxter's grin was not as prominent, but somewhat existent nonetheless. Butch Ed recognized Mookie as the boy down the road that he would see riding by on his bicycle every afternoon.

"Hello. We are the Fryes. I'm Stick, this is my wife, Hannah, and our boy, Mookie. We thought we would come by and welcome you to the neighborhood. We hope you like pineapple upside down cake. Hannah made it fresh this afternoon."

"Well, isn't that just the nicest thing! We sure do like that kind of cake and thank you ever so much for thinking of us enough to make it. I'm Butch Baxter. My wife here is Colleen and then we have a son, too. Butch Ed, shake Mr. Stick's hand."

Butch Ed stretched his hand toward Stick's outstretched hand, and the two wives smiled and nodded at each other. Hannah noted to herself that Colleen Baxter seemed shy. Sweet, but a bit shy.

Butch Baxter insisted that the Fryes stay and join them in having a piece of Hannah's cake.

"I believe this is the best pineapple upside down cake I have ever had, Miss Hannah." Butch Baxter was shoveling a second scoop of the cake into his mouth as he praised Hannah over her talents as a cake baker.

"Just Hannah is fine, Butch. You don't have to call me Miss Hannah. And thank you very much. I can't really take the credit for it though. I just received the recipe at our 4-H mom's meeting. My friend, Carole Harrington, is famous in these parts for her pineapple upside down cake. She was so kind to share the recipe with me. I will tell her that it was a big hit with the Baxter family."

"Well, then, Hannah, I will take that for what it's worth, but I won't back off from my admiration of your ability to throw it all together and get these amazing results." Butch Baxter continued to gush on and on about Hannah's cake. In fact, it was about to get a bit awkward until Stick changed the subject. Or at least tried to…

"How many head of cattle do you have here, Butch?" Stick was giving it his best effort.

"I'm running close to seventy now, but I'm buying another fifteen head from my father-in-law in Iowa. He's bringing them down here early next month, so I need to repair some of the fences before I can handle any more."

"Eighty-five will be a good number on the number of acres…" Butch interrupted Stick mid-sentence.

"Stick, I was just sitting here thinking to myself. You are such a lucky man. Your Hannah is not only a great cook, but she is beautiful to boot! Don't you think so, Colleen?"

All the Frye eyes shot a glance toward Colleen Baxter.

"He truly is a very lucky man, Butch. Beautiful wife that is a great cook." Colleen's voice trailed off, her face turned downward, and a strand of her bright red hair fell over her eyes. She seemed almost listless as she took another bite of the cake.

The awkwardness hung in the air like Spanish moss on a southern live oak tree until Stick made the first move to go home.

"Well, we need to get home. I have a few evening chores left and Mookie needs to feed the barnyard animals. Again, welcome to the community." Stick and Butch Baxter shook hands.

"Thanks so much for the cake and the company and thank you for being so gracious to welcome us to Blackjack Hollow. Hannah, maybe you and my Colleen can get together and swap recipes one of these days. Please include that cake recipe when you do." Butch Baxter followed the Fryes all the way to their truck, waving heartily as they drove away.

Later that evening, back at their house, Mookie overheard his mom and dad talking about the odd behavior of their new neighbors.

"What did you think, Stick? They seem like pretty nice people, but I just got a strange feeling all over me the longer we sat there."

"Well, Hannah, I know what you mean. That Butch Baxter seems like a very nice guy. Big smile. Big personality. He really liked your cake." They both giggled over that one. "Their son seemed like a good kid. He and Mookie hit it off right away. I don't know about Colleen, though. She seemed a little different. Like they didn't really match together or something. I can't quite put my finger on it. I guess we'll just have to wait and see."

"I agree. We will just have to wait and see. Oh and, Stick, I just had to laugh at that Butch Ed. Did you hear what he named his dog?"

"No, honey, I guess that was when I was having to listen to Butch rave on and on about your beauty and cake baking abilities." Stick smiled a teasing smile at Hannah as she rolled her eyes. "What did Butch Ed say about his dog?"

Hannah proceeded to tell Stick that when the blue heeler pup came into the Baxter's living room, Butch Ed Baxter said, "There's my dog." Mookie rushed over to the dog and started to pet him when he asked Butch Ed for the dog's name.

"My dog." Butch Ed said quite matter-of-factly.

"I know it's your dog, Butch Ed. What's his name?" Mookie questioned him again, thinking maybe he misunderstood what he had asked.

"That IS his name, Mookie. My dog's name is My Dog."

Hannah told Stick that Mookie laughed out loud as he continued to pat Butch Ed's pup on its head.

"Yep, we will have to wait and see on the Baxters, Hannah." Stick winked, and Hannah smiled.

CHAPTER 37:

Butch Ed's Summer to Remember

Mookie, Stoney, and Butch Ed became fast friends. Each summer, they loved riding their bicycles down the old dirt roads that surrounded their farms. Many hours into their latest escapade, they would oftentimes linger under the ancient trees that randomly deposited their dead branches on the ground. The boys would painstakingly gather the branches and attempt to build a fort at the base of the trees. The attempts never fully developed into a full-blown fort, as their stomachs usually signaled the need for lunch about a third of the way up, but it never stopped them from trying.

During their childhood, summertime in Oklahoma offered up an overabundance of hot, sultry days. Consequently, the trio rode their bikes at breakneck speed almost daily to the nearby spring-fed swimming hole.

Each of the three boys had chores they had to finish before they could head out for the day of exploring and playing. Mookie Frye's daily ritual consisted of feeding the barnyard animals and cleaning out the stalls. Stoney Allen couldn't start his adventures until he cleaned his hamster's cage and fed and watered the dogs. Butch Ed Baxter had been given the duty of mowing the lawn and weeding his mother's flower beds around the perimeter of their house.

The daily plan was to meet at Butch Ed's house after they were finished. Butch Ed lived closer to the swimming hole, allowing them to start their fun quicker if they left from his house.

It was a normal summer day. Mookie and Stoney's chores went smoothly, and they found themselves parked on their bikes in Butch Ed's front yard in record time.

It was a particularly dewy morning and Butch Ed was having a hard time with the power mower. The wet grass kept getting clogged underneath, killing the engine time and again. He had one last strip to finish before he could call it good, and it was becoming the most challenging one.

The Baxter's yard was fairly flat, with the exception of one grassy slope outside the kitchen door. Butch Ed's tennis shoes were covered in wet, slick, bermuda grass clippings, making it difficult for him to stand on the slope without slipping. He took his shoes off and banged them together hoping to get enough grass off them, so he could complete his mowing.

Blood spewed everywhere. It happened so fast. Mookie and Stoney jumped off their bikes as soon as they saw Butch Ed go down. Mookie ran inside to get Colleen Baxter and Stoney stayed with Butch Ed.

Butch Ed had not been able to get enough of the wet grass off the bottom of his shoes, therefore when he made the last run down the slope with the lawn mower, he slipped and both feet went directly underneath the spinning blades.

Mookie ran in the house and told Colleen what had happened. She hurried outside to Butch Ed, and Mookie called his mom to come help take them to the hospital.

When it was all said and done, the surgeon did the best he could to salvage as many toes as he could. Butch Ed ended up losing both big toes from his feet. He would have to learn to balance and walk differently without his big toes, but as kids normally do, he healed up quickly and was back swimming in the old swimming hole in record time.

CHAPTER 38

Mookie, P.I.

Mookie Frye's favorite television show was a crime drama series called Magnum, P.I. The handsome and debonair Tom Selleck portrayed Thomas Magnum, a Hawaii-based private investigator. Every Thursday night, Hannah would pop a big bowl of popcorn and she, Stick, and Mookie would tune in to see the latest episode.

Mookie loved watching how Magnum solved crimes and one evening as he was curled up on the couch next to his parents, watching Thomas Magnum, he got a brilliant idea. He would start his own P.I. business! Not only would he be available to investigate any future Bigfoot sightings, he could also see an opportunity to solve neighborhood crimes and misdemeanors. He wasn't real sure what a misdemeanor was, but he heard them say it on Magnum, P.I. so it must be important.

Mookie was making a mental note of his stash of private eye tools. He already had the bag of plaster of Paris that Henry and Dusty Waters left him before they headed back to Colorado. He was also sure that his mom had a bucket he could use, and best of all, Hannah had surprised

Mookie with his very own Polaroid 350. She had found it at their church rummage sale a couple of weeks ago. She bought the camera and six boxes of film for one dollar.

The very next day, Mookie went to the public library and asked his favorite librarian, Edwinna Blackworth, how much it would cost him to use the mimeograph machine to make copies of his business fliers.

"Mookie, I have a deal for you. If you can come here every day after school for one week and sweep the library floors, you can make as many fliers as you need."

After Mookie assured his parents that he would not neglect his regular after-school chores, they gave him the-go-ahead for his short stint as library floor sweeper.

Mookie, P.I. was now in business!

CHAPTER 39:

Going Forward with the Mission

Mookie distributed his Mookie, P.I. fliers to any business establishment that would let him tack one up on their bulletin board. Most of the business owners wished him the best with a tongue-in-cheek word of encouragement.

"We hope you catch the bad guys, Mookie. Our town can sure use a good private eye around here for all the unsolved crimes."

Mookie Frye was the talk of the town "spit and whittle club" that gathered at the local diner each morning for biscuits and gravy, and strong black coffee.

"That kid is so serious about this whole thing. I had to laugh when I read on his flier where it said that his services are free of charge. Too funny."

"Gotta hand it to him, though. He's wantin' to do somethin' good for the folks. Sounds like the feller has a really good heart. Although I'm thinkin' he's watchin' way too much tv."

Hearty chuckles went around the table, but the consensus ended up being that Mookie Frye was doing something they probably would have enjoyed doing if they were in the third grade again.

"Mookie! You have a telephone call.' Hannah Frye stepped out on her front porch and yelled toward the horse barn where her son, Mookie, was shoveling up piles of manure that were going to be added to the compost bin.

When Mookie heard his mom, he stuck his head out of the barn and asked her who was calling him on the telephone.

"It's the librarian, Mrs. Blackworth, Mookie." Hannah was motioning for Mookie to hurry to the house to take the call. Mookie propped his shovel against a post and headed toward the house.

"Hello. This is Mookie Frye."

"Good afternoon, Mookie. This is Edwinna Blackworth. I am calling to see if you wanted to test your private eye skills out this afternoon. I just spoke to your neighbor to the north, Mrs. Merriman. She was checking out some books when she proceeded to tell me that she is having a problem with something or someone stealing her chickens. I told her about your private investigation business and she asked me to contact you. What do you think?"

"Wow! That's great! Let me ask my mom and hopefully I will be right on it. Thank you for helping me get started, Mrs. Blackworth."

"You're very welcome, Mookie. I'm hoping that you will hone your skills enough to someday be able to find Bigfoot. You and I both believe that he is out there in those woods somewhere."

Mookie agreed with Edwinna. Bigfoot was out there and Mookie's main reason for his new venture was to learn as much as he could about following a trail, recognizing clues and gathering evidence. That's why he wasn't wanting to charge for his services. Mookie Frye was on a mission to eventually find Bigfoot.

He was truly a believer.

CHAPTER 40:

Then there was the Chicken Thief

Hannah called Mrs. Merriman and after a brief discussion about her chicken mystery, agreed to drive Mookie over to her place to start the investigation.

Mookie could hardly contain his excitement and had his private eye supplies loaded in the trunk of Hannah's car in no time.

"Mrs. Merriman, may I please dip some water from your rain barrel over there? I need it to put in my bucket of plaster of Paris."

"Why certainly, Mookie. Help yourself to as much as you need."

Mrs. Merriman and Hannah Frye watched with amazement as Mookie mixed his plaster of Paris to the correct consistency, and slowly poured the pancake batter looking substance into the paw prints that were scattered all around the ground in front of the door leading into the Merriman's chicken coop.

"Okay, Mom, I need to let this dry. Mrs. Merriman, I need to finish my chores. Mom can take me home to get them done and we will be back in about an hour to get the casts."

Hannah and Mrs. Merriman slowly shook their heads in agreement, not really understanding what exactly it was the Mookie was talking about when he said he would be coming back to get the casts. They guessed they would find out soon enough.

Hannah couldn't wait to tell Stick about how cute and professional Mookie was in his first investigation. More proud as she was for his determination to do a good job for Mrs. Merriman, she still didn't really understand that it was more to Mookie than just a fun thing to do. Hannah thought it was just a passing fancy brought on by too many episodes of Magnum, P.I. He would surely do this for a couple of times and then move on to something else.

Stick Frye, on the other hand, was impressed with Mookie's drive to do such a thorough job for Mrs. Merriman. He thought to himself that maybe Mookie was still thinking about Charley Bowman's Bigfoot sighting. Was Mookie just being a silly kid acting out a Magnum P.I. episode or was he as intrigued as Stick was with the possibility that Bigfoot could show himself again?

Stick was truly a believer.

CHAPTER 41:

The Casts Don't Lie

Mookie hurried as fast as he could to complete his afternoon chores so that he could get back to his casts in Mrs. Merriman's chicken pen.

He and Hannah met Mrs. Merriman at the gate after the allotted hour and proceeded to walk toward the white splats of plaster of Paris dotting the yard. Mookie used a popsicle stick to slowly lift the hardened plaster cast off the ground. Out of ten casts, Mookie was able to retrieve six good castings that clearly showed a defined paw print embedded into the plaster.

Mookie brought a cardboard box with him to the Merriman's farm and placed the plaster casts inside. He had cut pieces from used feed sacks and placed a layer of burlap in between each cast. Next, he pulled his Polaroid 350 instamatic camera from the satchel in Hannah's trunk, and walked around the crime scene taking pictures for further research.

CHAPTER 41: THE CASTS DON'T LIE

"Ok, Mrs. Merriman, I have everything I need to do my research and as soon as I get home I will look at our encyclopedias and see if I can figure out what made these prints. I will call you as soon as I can."

Hannah was so proud of how sweet her son was to Mrs. Merriman. Mrs. Merriman thanked them and said she would be anxious to see what he found out. Her husband had fallen from his tractor a week ago and was laid up with a bad back. She told them they were appreciative of any help they could get. She was already down seven chickens and she told Mookie and Hannah that they couldn't afford to lose more. She used her egg money to help with expenses on the farm and with Mr. Merriman being hurt, they were going to need all the money they could get.

"Look here, Mom. It's got to be a raccoon. The prints look exactly the same as the ones here in the book." Mookie was sitting at the kitchen table with his plaster casts spread around the encyclopedia. Hannah looked over his shoulder and saw that Mookie was right. The cast in the plaster of Paris looked just like the picture of a raccoon paw print in the photo in the Encyclopedia Britannica that was lying open on the table.

"Mystery solved, Mookie. I think you should call Mrs. Merriman with the news, so she can get her live traps set out this evening. Good job, son. I'm really proud of you." Hannah patted Mookie on his head and walked back over to the kitchen sink where she was peeling potatoes for supper.

"Your dad will be proud of you too, son." Hannah looked back at Mookie from her spot in front of the sink.

Mookie had just hung up the telephone after placing the call to Mrs. Merriman when Stick walked in the door from the garage. He had just finished setting bales of hay out for the cattle.

"Something smells good in this kitchen, Hannah. Are you making a roast? I am starving." Stick pulled out a kitchen chair from the table, sat down on it and began to take off his work boots.

"What's all this stuff out on the table? Mookie, you doin' a science project?"

"No, Dad, these are my plaster casts that I took over at the Merriman's farm. I just solved my first crime!" Mookie stuck his chest out and smiled a mile-wide grin at his father.

"Well, they sure are, Mookie! Looks like you did them just like the Waters boys showed you. What was the crime and who was the culprit?" Stick Frye picked up one of the plaster casts and held it up to the light to see the imprint of the paw print that was embossed in the white plaster.

"Chicken stealin', Dad. And the culprit was an old raccoon. Mrs. Merriman is gonna set out a live trap tonight to see if she can catch it."

Stick Frye looked over at his wife Hannah and they both grinned proudly at each other. There was nothing better than being the parents of such a sweet and cute kid like Mookie Frye. Nothing better at all.

CHAPTER 42:

Organizing the Efforts

Word of Mookie's private eye business spread quickly throughout the small community of Blackjack Hollow, Oklahoma. He began to get lots of calls about varmint mysteries on a weekly basis. He got so busy that it wasn't long before he recruited the help of his two best friends, Stoney Allen and Butch Ed Baxter.

The truth be known, most of the calls came from friends of friends that wanted to be nice to the three cute third graders. They weren't actually mysteries, but the folks didn't see the harm in letting the boys believe that they needed help with their critter problems.

The boys were having a blast and the "customers" enjoyed the show. It was truly a win-win.

Stick gave Mookie and his investigation team space in one of his sheds to store their crime scene evidence.

Mookie insisted that they kept thorough records of each investigation.

"Our first crime scene stored on this shelf will be the one that got me started on this mission." Mookie had placed the plaster casts that Dusty and Henry Waters had presented him, of a possible Bigfoot sighting, in a shoe box. He included with the prints all the written notes that he had taken as he followed the investigators from Colorado around Charley Bowman's farm. The description on the end of the box was simple. "Bigfoot was at Charley Bowman's Farm. Here's the proof."

As their investigations grew in number, they gathered old shoe boxes and filled them with evidence of each crime, writing the description on the end of each box, where it would be visible for future reference.

Over the years, as the boys got older, they branched out their investigative efforts to include actual crime or accident scene evidence recovery. They kept this part of their investigative work to themselves. They swore each other to secrecy and were very careful not to interfere with any law enforcement investigations and would wait until they were satisfied that the area was no longer being actively searched. Sometimes, however, they didn't wait as long, as their curiosity got the better of them. They would go to crime scenes after the local law enforcement officers went home for the day and make a few quick plaster casts, carefully, as not to disturb the site.

Several boxes were marked, "Cow Thief Footprints and Pictures -Markham Farm- July 16, 1984", and "Car Wreck – Footprints and Pictures – December 13, 1985," "Vandalism- Methodist Church – March 18, 1985", just to name a few.

They didn't keep those boxes out in the open like they did the others. The true crime scene boxes were hidden at the back of the shelf. Out of sight. The boys didn't think they were actually doing anything wrong, they just had the feeling that they probably should let this be a secret held between three of them.

For now, anyway.

CHAPTER 43:

It was Bound to Happen

After several summers on the town Little League teams and by the time Mookie hit junior high, it was inevitable. He was full blown ate up with rodeo and baseball fever. Just like his dad - and he was extremely talented too. Just like his dad.

Stick already knew his kid was a natural athlete by the time he was out of diapers. He could swing a bat, hit a ball, and run like the dickens when he was on his first Pee Wee League baseball team at six years old. As for bull riding, Stick made Mookie his own rope and tire bull, and of course, they named him Tooty Frooty 2. Mookie could hang solid on ol' Tooty Frooty 2. Just like a stick-tight burr. Stick thought he would burst with pride when his son's athletic abilities were on full display.

Memories of days gone by often surfaced for Stick Frye. Good memories. Every single one of them. Seeing his talented son, Mookie, perfecting his baseball skills and seeing the excitement on his son's young face when they would head out to the nearest rodeo to watch the bull riders give it their best shots to hang for eight was nothing short of a miracle. It put the biggest smile on Stick's face, and pride in his heart to see Mookie having such a good time. It was unfortunate that Stick didn't get to live his own dream, but he never felt sorry for himself. He had vowed that he would not raise a fist to God and say, "why me, Lord?" That was not how Boots Frye's son would live his life. Stick vowed that he would thank God profusely for every blessing that was within his grasp. Every day of his life was precious for Stick. Every single day of his life was a gift. That El Diablo could have ended everything for Stick Frye in the middle of the arena in Muskogee, Oklahoma. He came very close to dying that night and he never doubted it for a minute. He was still alive for a reason. Stick figured that God wasn't through with him yet and he would be danged if he thought for a minute that he was disappointing God, or the memory of his dad, Boots. Boots Frye, the best dad ever.

Stick wanted to be the best dad ever to his son and he often prayed that Boots Frye was looking down from heaven, proud of the man that Stick had become. Stick Frye's desire was to be the best dad ever.

Watching Mookie excel in sports put Stick smack dab on top of the world. Pain or no pain, he wasn't going to let the stinking reminders of that horrible accident years ago steal his joy. He loved his wife and son with everything in him, and he was blessed to have a farm that gave him immense pleasure every time he saw a newborn calf snuggling at the feet of its momma. Stick Frye was determined to make the best of his life. These were the cards he had been dealt and nothing was going to change the past. His doctor in Tulsa was doing a pretty fair job with keeping his pain under control and Stick Frye had no complaints. He was a blessed man. No doubt about that.

His current mission was to enter Mookie in all the junior rodeos around northeastern Oklahoma they could find, and to see that he was on a good Little League baseball team. Stick would have to work double time to keep the farm going in the upcoming summer, but he knew it would be worth the extra hard work to give his boy every opportunity he could to excel in the sports that he loved. It didn't hurt a bit that Stick Frye was the perfect "personal" coach for Mookie. What better person than Stick Frye to show Mookie the ropes in firing a baseball with exacting precision over home plate or instruct him on the best techniques for hanging on for the full eight seconds atop a feisty bull.

CHAPTER 44:

Big League Chew

There was not another kid in the state that had the pitching statistics that were as off the chart as those being plastered up by Mookie Frye. He was a phenomenal athlete and the joke around town was wondering how soon his parents would take out a one-million-dollar insurance policy on his arm. He could rock and fire a baseball with pinpoint accuracy and his speed was off the clock.

It was a common occurrence to see scouts sitting in the local stands from the St. Louis Cardinals and his favorite team of all, just like his dad, the Kansas City Royals. The Oklahoma State Cowboys, and the Oklahoma Sooners were sending coaches his way too, as were many of the state's junior colleges. Mookie was tremendously humbled. He just wanted to make his dad proud.

One early spring day, Hannah was sweeping the front porch when a postal truck pulled up in their driveway. The mail carrier jumped out with a medium sized box and headed up toward the Frye's house.

"Good afternoon, Mrs. Frye. I have a package here. It's addressed to Stick." As all small-town news is the big news of the day, "and it says on the return label it's coming all the way from Los Angeles, California. It looks mighty impressive to me."

Hannah giggled under her breath, took the package, and facetiously thanked the postman for his trouble and for his keen eye.

"I'm sure it's something really important." Hannah smiled as she attempted to placate the nosy postman, turning to walk back up the porch steps and into the house.

"Big League Chew Corporation. What in the world in this?" Hannah sat the box on the kitchen table. She was extremely curious but decided to wait and let Stick open it when he came in from checking the cows. "Hmm, it sure is from Los Angeles."

Mookie and Hannah stood behind Stick as he took his pocket knife and cut a slit in the top of the box that had found its way to Blackjack Hollow, Oklahoma from Los Angeles, California.

The excitement mounted as he pulled apart the flaps, especially when they saw an envelope taped to a piece of cardboard that had been placed on top of the contents of the box.

"To Stick Frye, son of one of the greatest men on earth."

Stick used his pocket knife again to open the top of the envelope to expose a hand-written letter. He read it aloud to his family.

"Hello, Stick. I don't know if you remember me or not. I'm an old friend of your dad's. We go way, way back. All the way to elementary school. Your dad has been on my mind a lot lately. I believe I admired him above anyone else I've ever known. I sure miss him, and I know you do too. He used to keep me filled in on your talents in baseball and rodeo when you were growing up. I was always proud for him and proud of you. I am hearing through the grapevine that you have a son that is carrying on the Frye name with glory and is getting recognition all around the countryside. I know you are proud. With that said, I wanted to honor your dad's memory, your past accomplishments, and, since your Mookie is making a name for himself as a standout left-handed pitcher, inside this box is a new product that a friend of mine that works for the Wrigley Company, has started marketing. It's a brand of bubble gum, called Big League Chew. Rob Nelson, the left-handed pitcher for the Portland Mavericks created it as a fun alternative to chewing tobacco. The top carton has been opened. All the packages in that one have each been signed by the entire Portland Mavericks baseball team. Tell Mookie to enjoy the bubble gum, to stuff his cheeks to the brim, and rock and fire all the stuff he's got right over that plate! Best regards to the Frye family, Pete Hollister."

Stick, Hannah, and Mookie's eyes lit up as each carton of Big League Chew was carefully lifted out of the box. Mookie's attention went directly to the one that had the packages signed by the baseball team.

"Dad, look! Each one of the packages that is signed has my name on it! Oh wow!"

Mookie found a special place on a shelf on his bedroom wall to place the autographed packages of Big League Chew. He loved showing them off to his friends. He would treasure them forever, and as directed by Mr. Pete Hollister, Mookie stuffed his cheek full of the shredded bubble gum each time he walked on the baseball mound to pitch. It became his signature trait.

CHAPTER 45:

Mookie and the ACRA Finals

The American Cowboy Rodeo Association had always had a strong presence in the northeastern parts of Oklahoma. Thus, in December of 1985, the finals were to be held nearby in Springfield, Missouri.

When Stick and Hannah were attending college in Miami, Oklahoma, Hannah made fast friends with a girl in several of her classes, Marilyn Maple. Even after Stick and Hannah moved away from Miami, they stayed in contact with her and her family, and like the Fryes, the Maples were a hardcore rodeo family.

"Mookie, I'm taking you and your momma to Springfield, Missouri this weekend to see the ACRA finals. Do you remember our friend that we see at the rodeos, Marilyn Maple?"

"I do, Dad. I remember her." Mookie couldn't contain his enthusiasm. The thought of getting to go to the ACRA finals was a dream come true.

"Well, we're excited for Marilyn. She is a finalist in the barrel racing this year and your momma and I want to go watch her. How does that sound?" Stick Frye was beaming at his teenage son. He knew that Mookie was thrilled to get to go to the finals.

The rodeo season of 1985 had been the best junior rodeo season to date for Mookie Frye. He had been posting wins all over the youth rodeo circuit in the area, reminiscent of his dad when he was Mookie's age. The rodeo world was beginning to take notice of the teenager and Stick Frye couldn't be prouder of his son.

Since early spring, Mookie had been entered in contests in a round indoor arena in Tulsa, a small indoor arena in Chewy, Oklahoma (named humorously by the locals, The Chewy Dome), and the place he posted the most wins, Ochelata, Oklahoma. There was a lot of activity in the junior rodeo world in Ochelata and Mookie had been claiming the majority of the prizes awarded in that arena.

Mookie's collection of belt buckles and saddles was beginning to rival that of his dad's and a trip to the ACRA finals was a fitting high point to the year-end of rodeoing for the Frye family.

A motel was booked, their truck was loaded with their luggage, and the Frye family headed out for the three-hour drive to Springfield, Missouri.

The action-packed, three-day weekend found them sitting in the bleachers watching the best of the best of the rodeo cowboys and cowgirls in the area. The excitement was never ending. Mookie didn't want to miss an event as he was in awe of every single aspect of rodeoing and Stick and Hannah were just as thrilled to be there.

By Friday afternoon, Mookie made his way back up the bleachers where his parents were sitting. It was time for the Cowgirl's Barrel Racing semi-finals and Mookie's run to the concession stand had them well stocked with plenty of hot dogs, potato chips, Tootsie Roll Pops, and the newest release from the makers of Coca Cola, Cherry Cokes. Stick, Hannah, and Mookie had arrived early and found good seats in the bleachers where they could get a bird's eye view.

"It looks like Marilyn races fourth today." Stick had the ACRA program in his good hand, and a Tootsie Roll Pop in the other as he read the statistics for the day's Cowgirl Barrel Races.

Stick explained to Mookie that the year's top fifteen racers got to go to the ACRA finals. The fastest time each day won that go and the fastest time of all three days was the finals champion.

"It looks like she is one of the older ones out there. I see the youngest is 15 and the oldest one is 40. Dang, it sure says a lot for Marilyn. A woman in her thirties being here competing with teenagers." Stick said as he pointed out Marilyn's statistics in the program to Hannah.

After a standing ovation for all the veterans in attendance, the audience's attention turned to the announcers.

"First up is Stevie Sue Wilcox. She's on a little roan named Hank. They've got the barrels all set up. You know, Sam, these riders can't see the first barrel until they come out of the alley and come in to the arena. Left barrel first! Here she goes!"

The first two racers posted decent times, 14.6 and 15.2. The third racer came in with a flat 16, knocking over two barrels in the race.

Stick, Hannah, and Mookie stood up when the announcers prepared the crowd for Marilyn's race. They happened to look to their left and saw her husband and her kids waving at them. The Fryes flashed them a "thumbs up" and huge smiles for Marilyn.

"Marilyn Maple has had a remarkable year. She's currently tops in the money and if she makes a good run here in Springfield, we might be looking at this year's ACRA champion and Year End champ. She brings with her a familiar guy. That's her red line back dun, Dunny. He's a spectacular animal. Comin' out of the alley is Marilyn Maple, from Miami, Oklahoma!"

The duo of Marilyn Maple and her steed, Dunny was a sight to see. They flew around the barrels with such a perfect pattern, the crowd rose to their feet. It was a horserace home, putting them in a solid lead.

At the end of the weekend, Mookie had seen every event choose a champion. He sat in amazement as he watched bronc riders, ropers, and his favorite of all, bull riding. Stick gave a play by play of each bull rider, giving Mookie pointers as he went. Mookie had a first-hand look at the best bull riders around and was ready to try some of the new techniques he had learned.

The highlight of the rodeo was, hands down, the fact that their friend, Marilyn Maple, won the 1985 ACRA Cowgirl's Barrel Race champion, with the best time of 13.9, and being top in the earnings, making her the 1985 Year End Cowgirl's Barrel Race champion.

It was the time of his life, and Mookie didn't stop talking about everything he had seen the entire three hours home.

Marlene and the Legacy

Mookie Frye continued to dominate the junior rodeo circuit in and around the tri-state area. Spring and summertime in Kansas, Oklahoma, and Missouri, offered up as many events as the Fryes could squeeze into their schedules. Mookie's baseball, rodeos, and a few trips to Kansas City to see their beloved Royals, filled every spare moment of their time. Stick, Mookie, and Hannah, chipped in to keep the farm chores caught up, as they were like a well-oiled machine, all for the love of baseball and rodeos.

The Loopers and his grandmother, Marlene Frye, attended as many of Mookie's events as they could. He was never happier than when he looked up in the stands and saw his family up on their feet, cheering and clapping for their Mookie Frye.

One particular weekend, in Shawnee, Oklahoma, Mookie held a solid lead in the bull riding event going in to the Saturday night finals.

The family had chosen a popular Chinese restaurant for lunch prior to heading to the rodeo grounds.

The owner of the restaurant came over to their table and before long, had the entire family in stitches as he peppered them with funny one-liners.

"They call me the Johnny Carson of Japan," he said with a toothy grin.

The food was delicious. After the last bite of Asian cuisine was finished and the last fork was set back down on the table, Marlene Frye stood up.

"Mookie, I want you to know that I brought something for you today. I have been waiting for the right moment to do this, and after talking to your mom and learning your shoe size, now is the time to give these to you." Marlene reached down and brought up a paper sack. She handed the sack to Stick, who in turn passed it across the table to Mookie.

Mookie reached into the sack and brought up a pair of cowboy boots. Embossed in the leather in the front of the boot were the two letters, "BF". Everyone sitting around the table knew immediately that the boots had belonged to Mookie's granddad, Boots Frye.

"Oh my gosh, Grandma. I don't know what to say. These are granddad's. I'm so honored." Mookie brought the pair of boots up close to his chest. He was beaming with pride. Stick walked around the table and placed his good arm around his son's shoulders. A steady stream of tears trickled down both of their cheeks.

"Well, Mookie. It looks like you are all set now. You can carry on your granddad's legacy. I am so proud of you." Stick continued to hug his son as he beamed with pride at the moment that so aptly honored his late father, Boots.

Mookie hurried over to Marlene and scooped up his grandmother and swung her around in a big bear hug. It was a very happy occasion for the entire family.

"Dad, and Grandma, if it's okay, I would like to wear these tonight. I just know they will be my good luck charms."

Mookie didn't even wait for the-go-ahead before he sat down and proceeded to take off his boots and replace them with his granddad's special boots.

It was a perfect fit!

Mookie won the bull riding event hands-down that evening, and never stepped foot into another rodeo arena without his lucky "BF" leather embossed cowboy boots.

CHAPTER 47:

Colleen Baxter's Midnight Ride

Mookie, Stoney Allen and Butch Ed Baxter, were inseparable friends. If you came across one, you would see the other two.

From the very beginning of their friendship, it was obvious they were fiercely loyal to each other and didn't mind showing it at all. Stoney and Butch Ed had heard the story about why Mookie's dad, Stick, walked with a profound limp and the reason behind why he didn't have the full use of his right arm. Stick Frye was a hero in their eyes and they would never stand by idly and listen to anyone tease their best friend, Mookie, about his dad's disabilities.

In addition, Mookie and Butch Ed would give the stink eye to any kid that even hinted at bad-mouthing Stoney's dad, Satch. Satch Allen was the high school principal and not only was it a very challenging position, situations often led to wagging tongues and dissatisfied parents griping about the "unfair" treatment of their "angels." Mookie and Butch

Ed knew every one of those "angels" and as far as they were concerned, the halos on those kids' heads needed a lot of polishing.

The same allegiance was extended toward Butch Ed. They were just kids, but it didn't take a rocket scientist to know that things at the Baxter house were off kilter. Way off kilter.

Without a doubt, Mookie and Stoney came from loving families and from the displays of open affection, it was obvious their parents' marriages were solid and harmonious. Unfortunately for Butch Ed Baxter, the same couldn't be said for Butch and Colleen Baxter. On several occasions, when Mookie and Stoney would ride up to the Baxter home on their bicycles, they could hear the yelling and screaming that seemed to rattle the rafters. More than once, they would witness Butch Baxter come blowing out the front door, slamming the screen door loudly behind him. Without acknowledging the two wide-eyed youngsters sitting on their bikes with their mouths hanging open, Butch would jump in his truck and drive away, leaving a trail of dust in his wake.

"Bye, Mom. I'm going bike riding with Mookie and Stoney. Will you be all right?" Mookie and Stoney heard Butch Ed's voice inside the house, but Colleen Baxter's was just a faint mumble. Butch Ed would come bounding out on the front porch as if nothing was wrong.

"Let's go, guys. I have some pieces of cardboard in the garage. Let's go get them and ride over by the overpass and slide down the hill."

Even though they were glad that Butch Ed didn't seem sad, it troubled them, nonetheless, that he didn't act sad and that was unsettling to Mookie and Stoney. They felt bad for their friend and they would be loyal to him no matter what.

The "what" of "no matter what" came sooner than expected.

The telephone on Stick and Hannah's kitchen wall seemed to be ringing with an urgent intensity. It was midnight and Stick was trying to wake up as he hurried to pick up the receiver. He prayed that it wasn't something wrong with his mom. Marlene Frye was living in Broken Arrow, Oklahoma in the same neighborhood as her cousins, Harriet and Bud Looper. She had been a little under the weather and Stick immediately started beating himself up over not going to see her and check on her often enough. "Please, God, let this not be about my mom."

"Stick! Please come over. Can you get over here right away? Oh my God! Colleen's…Oh my God, Stick. Colleen is dead."

Butch Baxter's first phone call was to his neighbor and friend, Stick Frye. The second phone call was to the sheriff.

Hannah was sitting up in bed as Stick threw on his clothes.

"I will try to let you know what's going on as soon as I can. If Mookie wakes up, you can go ahead and tell him. I might be bringing Butch Ed back with me." Stick leaned over and gave Hannah a kiss on the cheek. She reached up and placed her hand on his shoulder.

"Be careful, honey."

When Stick drove up to the Baxter's house, there were two deputies standing in the yard next to their patrol cars. The lights were flashing a constant pattern of red and blue.

Stick jumped out of his truck, barely getting it in gear before he shut the engine off.

"Where's Butch?"

It was pitch dark in the yard, except for the flashing lights. It took the two officers a second to see that the person hurrying toward them was Stick Frye.

169

"Hello, Stick. Butch and Sheriff Stonecipher went over to the bluffs by the lake to take a look at the wreckage. How did you know about this?"

"There was a wreck? This late at night? So, Colleen died in a car wreck, is that what you're tellin' me? Butch called me and told me she was dead, but I didn't know that it was a wreck."

"Well, maybe we better rephrase that. It wasn't a wreck, per se. There's wreckage, mind you, but it looks like a suicide. Her car went over a cliff. Smelled of beer. Sheriff Stonecipher says it looks like she hit her head when the car landed at the bottom. We just got here and were getting ready to check and see if there's anyone in the house."

Stick was trying hard to process what he had just heard from the deputy. Colleen got drunk and drove herself over a cliff? In the middle of the night?

"Let me go up there and make sure their boy, Butch Ed, isn't in there by himself. He's just a teenager." Stick stepped around the two deputies and headed toward the Baxter's house.

As he mounted the first step on the Baxter's porch, he could see the faint glow of a lamp in the living room. Before Stick had a chance to knock on the door, he peered through the picture window and saw Butch Ed sitting on the couch with his head in his hands. Stick decided to go on in without knocking. He told himself that he was surprised that the kid had been left at the house by himself. He must be scared to death.

Stick Frye walked softly from the front foyer into the living room where Butch Ed was sitting. He heard a soft whimper coming from the boy.

"Butch Ed, are you okay?" Stick leaned over and put his hand on the boy's shoulder.

"Get out of here and leave me alone. I mean it. Go away!" Butch Ed Baxter looked up at Stick with a scowl as he jerked his body away from Stick's hand.

"Butch Ed, I know you're scared and sad. Why don't you let me take you over to our house? You can bunk with Mookie."

"Get out of my house. I don't want to go anywhere. Just leave me alone." Butch Ed Baxter jumped up and headed up the stairs to his room.

Stick found himself standing alone in the Baxter's living room. Butch Ed's reaction was somewhat understandable, the kid had just lost his mom. Nevertheless, Stick Frye had a very uneasy feeling about the entire situation. Profound grief was not the sentiment he saw in Butch Ed Baxter's eyes. It was furor. Unleashed and unabashed. Unholy furor.

CHAPTER 48:

Case Closed

Colleen Baxter's death was deemed a suicide. As he sat humped over in Sheriff Stonecipher's office, Butch Baxter dabbed his weeping eyes with a bandana as he painfully described his recently deceased wife as a closet alcoholic, hellbent on self-destruction. A box of Kleenex was sympathetically pushed toward the grieving widower as he ticked off the events leading up to the fateful night she was discovered to be unresponsive in the wreckage of her car. The events of the evening that found her in a drunken state as she careened her car off the cliff. He sobbed and told them that he woke up and found her side of the bed empty and her car gone from the garage. He recounted how he drove for hours looking for her, only to find her lifeless body in the tangled mess that was her car. "Our son is devastated. I don't know how to help him deal with the loss of his mother." The entire staff sitting at their desks in the sheriff's office, lowered their heads with sadness for the pitiful man.

The cause of Colleen Baxter's death was logged on her death certificate as blunt force trauma to the head. Bloody strands of her hair were enmeshed in the broken windshield glass in her upside-down car at the bottom of the canyon. Empty beer cans were scattered in the passenger seat and a few cans were scattered in the leaves outside the car, apparently having flown out the window upon impact.

The case was cut and dried. It was what it was, and the folder labeled "Colleen Baxter" was methodically tucked away without dispute.

The next morning after Colleen Baxter's accident, Charley Bowman finished his sunrise cup of coffee, set the cup in the sink, and headed out for his Saturday ritual of checking to see if the food he had left in the wash pan the night before was gone. As he crept up to the tree stump, he could see the pan sitting in plain sight. The food he had left in it was gone and inside the aluminum wash pan Charley saw an upright and empty beer can. "Is this from you, Bigfoot?" Charley wondered perceptibly. He stuck the can in his pocket and headed back home.

Five days after local law enforcement investigated the area surrounding Colleen Baxter's smashed up vehicle, Mookie Frye and Stoney Allen slid a cardboard box behind some other boxes on their private eye shelf. It was filled with plaster casts, and other items gathered from the scene of the wreckage of Colleen Baxter's car. They labeled it "CB Wreck" and never mentioned it again.

CHAPTER 49:

The Transformation of Butch Ed Baxter

It was difficult for Mookie and Stoney to understand how to deal with the undoing of their friendship with their buddy, Butch Ed Baxter. They were very sorry for him that he lost his mom and wanted nothing more than to be there for their friend as he grieved her death, but sadly, he pushed them away. Not only did he not want to be friends with them anymore, he also became bitter and hateful toward them. No matter how hard they tried, Butch Ed was relentless in his desire to terminate the friendship.

Several times they rode their bicycles to his house to see if he would come on a ride with them. Each time Butch Ed would come flying out of the farmhouse, slamming the screen door behind him.

"Get out of my yard! I mean it. Don't you ever come to my house again. Leave me alone!"

Subsequently, after Colleen's death, Butch Baxter spent a lot of time with Stick and Hannah. They were glad to be able to be a friend to him in his time of sorrow and welcomed him to their home on many occasions for supper, and a game of spades, dominoes or Uno. However, no matter how hard they tried to get him to come, if Butch Baxter drove over to the Frye farm for a visit, his son Butch Ed never came with him. Stick and Hannah continued to offer sympathy and advice to Butch on different ways to help Butch Ed rekindle the friendship between the three boys, but Butch assured them that there was nothing they or anyone could do for Butch Ed.

Nonetheless, Butch Baxter thanked Stick and Hannah profusely for caring enough to want to help his son. "I'm pretty much at a loss. He's taking the death of his mother very, very hard. I've tried to get him counseling but he won't cooperate at all. He's one hard headed kid. A lot like his mom."

CHAPTER 50:

Mookie's Bandwagon

Boots Frye never had another drink after his wife Marlene gave him the ultimatum. He spent the rest of his life telling his son, Stick, to steer clear of alcohol. Boots Frye's mantra was simple. "Alcohol is evil and can ruin your life". He never went into any details about why he hated the concoction so badly, he just preached over and again that it was wicked.

On the other hand, Stick Frye was upfront with his son Mookie, from the time he was knee high to a grasshopper, the whole story about his battle with pain from the accident, and how the effects of alcohol almost lost him his marriage and his son. He didn't leave any detail to the imagination. He told Mookie that even if he had thought alcohol helped him forget the pain for a very short amount of time, it also made him stupid, worthless, ugly, and did he say stupid?

Stick's rebuking of alcohol struck a chord with his son. When Mookie Frye reached high school, it was a well-known fact that if you hung around him for any length of time at all, you would get a lecture about the stupidity of getting drunk on alcohol.

Chapter 50: Mookie's Bandwagon

Mookie Frye was popular, and well-liked in his hometown. Even though many of his high school friends chose to drink, they were respectful enough to listen to Mookie's pleas to be responsible. They knew he was passionate about it, and they remained courteous to him, out of total respect for him as a good person.

Mookie was also very proud of his dad. Stick Frye's battle with pain was a constant in his life, but he was strong in his faith in God, and he stuck to his convictions to never touch alcohol again in his life. Pain or no pain, he wanted to be the best husband and father to Hannah and Mookie, and he spent every day of his life showing his love and devotion to them both.

Hence, his family was Stick's motivation to find alternatives to focusing on his pain. One of the best stress and pain relievers for Stick Frye was spending time on his old tractor. He called her Gertie, and he often told Mookie and Hannah that even on his worst days, he seemed to forget his pain when he would climb into the cab of his tractor, start the old girl up, and tool around doing his farm work for hours on end. Motoring around in Gertie and spending time with God. Two of Stick's favorite stress relievers.

Stick Frye was such a good man and Hannah and Mookie Frye adored him. They never once doubted that he was doing everything he did out of love for them.

Things Aren't Always as they Seem

The contest between the two American Legion summer baseball league teams saw Mookie's team claim victory with a shut-out in a stand up, sit down showdown. Each inning, Mookie Frye coolly sashayed to the pitcher's mound, looking down at his feet as he placed them perfectly on the rubber. Slowly and methodically looking up, tugging the front of his ball cap further down on his brow, he nodded in agreement to the signals from the catcher, Stoney Allen. Time after time, Mookie steadfastly caressed the leather of the baseball, zoning in on the exact spot on the threads to hurl pitch after pitch past each helmeted head on the opposing team's roster. As the ball hummed past each batter, Stick whispered to Hannah that the batters looked like they were swatting flies.

Stick and Hannah were proudly in the stands as their son, Mookie, wowed the crowd with his record-breaking afternoon on the baseball field. It couldn't have been a more perfect performance for Mookie.

CHAPTER 51: THINGS AREN'T ALWAYS AS THEY SEEM

"Hannah, don't look now, but this is incredible. Okay, you can look now. Over there by the third base line." Stick could hardly contain his excitement. "That, my dear, is the manager for the Kansas City Royals. It's John Wathan. I betcha he's here to scout Mookie, and by golly, he's getting exactly what he came for."

Stick and Hannah glowed. They were pretty sure Mookie knew he was there too. The Fryes knew everything there was to know about their favorite baseball team. They loved the Kansas City Royals with a passion.

"Mookie's cool as a cucumber. That's one thing that he's not like me. I was always a nervous wreck when I was being scouted. Ol' Mook is like steel out there." Stick laughed and squeezed Hannah's hand.

At the end of the game, Mookie gathered his baseball glove and bat and made a beeline for his parents.

"Did you see John Wathan? Oh my gosh, I was freaking out." A breathless Mookie was grinning ear to ear. "Do you think he liked how I pitched?"

Stick and Hannah both answered their son with a resounding "Yes!"

After a celebratory supper in town, the Fryes headed back home.

"I'm goin' to plow a bit before the sun goes down, Hannah. There's rain comin' and I don't wanna miss the opportunity to get the ground ready for sowin' the winter wheat."

Stick placed a tender kiss on his wife's cheek and headed out to mount ol' Gertie. Hannah had some embroidery work she wanted to finish, and Mookie was all set to watch "The Wonder Years" on the family's television in the living room.

A few hours later, Hannah stuck her head in the living room where Mookie was sprawled out on the floor, sound asleep.

"Mook, Mookie. Wake up, son. I guess we both fell asleep. I just woke up and realized your dad is still in the field. Come on and we'll drive out there and see if we can find him. Gertie might be broken down out there." Mookie jumped right up, rubbing his eyes, and headed for his shoes over by the couch.

Before Hannah could grab the keys to the truck and start out the back door with Mookie, they heard loud banging on the front door.

Through the lace curtains, Hannah could faintly see two men on her front porch. She and Mookie were standing side by side as she opened the front door.

It was Sheriff Stonecipher and Butch Baxter. Their faces said it all.

"Hannah, can we come in? We have some bad news for you."

Hannah and Mookie moved like tin soldiers toward the hallway.

Butch spoke first.

"Hannah. Hannah, I was out checkin' my cows. They were bawlin' and bellerin' and I went out to see what the commotion was. There was a coyote out there snoopin' around my new born calves. Well, anyway, Hannah, oh my God. Well, Hannah, I chased off the coyote and then I saw a light off in the distance. It was over on your place, so I drove over there to take a look."

Sheriff Stonecipher interrupted Butch.

"Mrs. Frye. I am so sorry to tell you this. Stick rolled the tractor and was pinned underneath. I'm sorry to have to be the one to tell you this, Hannah. Stick is dead."

Hannah collapsed into Mookie's arms.

Butch placed his hand on Hannah's back. "Hannah, I am so very sorry. I don't even know what to say. This is so terrible. Mookie, son, my heart is breaking for you two. Whatever I can do to help. You know you can count on me."

Sheriff Stonecipher explained to Mookie and Hannah that the coroner was on his way to the scene of the accident. He advised them to not go out there. He told them that they did not want to have the gruesome scene in their minds for the rest of their lives. "He wouldn't want you two to see him like that."

Even though Mookie pleaded with his mother to let him go with Sheriff Stonecipher to the field where his dad lay dead, she refused to allow him to go.

Butch Baxter lingered after Sheriff Stonecipher went to his car. He put his hand on Mookie's shoulder and turned to speak to Hannah.

"Hannah, maybe you should sit down. I'm sorry to tell you this, but there were signs of alcohol. I'm so sorry."

Hannah and Mookie were devastated and confused. Alcohol? Did Butch Baxter say that alcohol was involved in the accident? They couldn't believe what they were hearing. Stick Frye hadn't had a drop of alcohol to drink since the day he found out he was going to be a father. Or had he? Did he drink secretively? They could not wrap their minds around any of this.

Stick was gone, and they felt like they were too.

CHAPTER 52

Mookie's Visitors

Five days later, Hannah and Mookie Frye sat in the first pew of the First United Methodist Church in Tishomingo, Oklahoma, for the final farewell to their beloved Stick Frye. They were surrounded by Stick's mother, Marlene, the Loopers, and a multitude of family, friends, and acquaintances, all heart-broken at the loss of such a fine human being.

Following the funeral, they gathered in the Fellowship Hall of the church for lunch. The ladies of the congregation prepared a wonderful home-cooked meal, and the afternoon was spent reminiscing about the lives of Stick and his father, Boots. Marlene had set up a table in the back of the hall piled high with newspaper clippings, trophies, pictures, posters, and all sorts of memorabilia that listed the impressive accomplishments of her late husband, Boots, and her beloved son, Stick. The two fine men left a powerful legacy.

Mookie's heart swelled with pride as he lovingly picked up every single item on the table, read each clipping, and touched each memento, trophy, and keepsake. He vowed to do everything in his power to live the kind of life that his grandfather and dad lived. They were honorable, loving, devoted, Christian men. He didn't want to ever let them down.

As he held a picture of himself and his dad, the tears rolled endlessly down his cheeks, pooling up on his chin, then sliding slowly down his neck. He was in his Little League uniform and Stick was standing next to him with his left arm around his son. They were both beaming at the camera. There were no pictures of Stick and Mookie with Stick standing on the Mookie's left side. Stick always walked around Mookie to be on the side where his good arm could hold his son tightly.

"How am I gonna do this, Dad? I need you here. I wanted you to be here forever. I wanted you to stay here." Mookie's hushed pleas were directed at the man in the picture. His dad. His rock. Mookie knew deep down that he would never fail to be there for his mom. His dad would expect him to see that she was taken care of for the rest of her life and Mookie vowed to never let his dad down.

Even though he felt let down.

Mookie felt so let down by God. Why did something so bad happen to someone so good? He was overcome by his grief. He truly wanted to hit somebody.

"Mookie, are you ready to go home? I think I've had about as much of this as I can stand." It was his mom. Hannah wrapped her arm around her son's waist as he stood by the table with a face full of a river of tears.

"How are we gonna do this, Mom?"

"Mookie, you and I come from a long line of strong folks. Good folks. There's no doubt about that. Look at this table. It is filled with the everlasting legacy of your granddad and your daddy. Neither one of these men ever gave up on anything that ever came their way. They were fighters to the very end. You and I will do whatever it takes to make them know someday that we didn't squander their legacy. Fryes are fighters and you and I know that God is in this with us. We don't know why things like this happen. I just know we aren't supposed to know all the answers. Now, here's a Kleenex. Wipe your face. We're taking your grandma home with us for a couple of weeks, so go get her red suitcase out of Uncle Bud and Aunt Harriet's car and put it in our truck. Then, I want you to come back with a smile on your face, say a gracious goodbye to everyone, grab your grandmother by the hand and help her outside to our truck. We've got a farm to run."

The long ride from Tishomingo, Oklahoma to Blackjack Hollow, Oklahoma turned out to be just what the three of them needed. Marlene shared stories about Stick that neither Hannah nor Mookie had ever heard. The stories were mostly funny, so it did their souls good to have the sound of laughter filling the vehicle.

Marlene fell sound asleep in the backseat about an hour from home, leaving Mookie and Hannah sitting in a period of silence in the front seat. They were exhausted, both mentally and physically.

Hannah's voice was the first to pierce the quiet.

"Mookie, I don't want you to dwell on what Butch said about your dad and the alcohol. Your daddy wouldn't want us to be tormented by thoughts like that. We need to just go on the best we know how, and always remember what a wonderful man he was. He had so much pain…"

"I won't, Mom. I won't, but I'm never gonna stop hating alcohol. Ever." Mookie stared off into the night with a fierce resolve. Hannah left it there, as they rode the rest of the way, deep in their own thoughts.

Hannah maneuvered the truck into their driveway around midnight. Mookie helped his grandmother, Marlene, into the house, leading her into the guest bedroom. He hoisted her large red suitcase onto a table by the window and looked around the room to make sure all was in good order and ready to make his grandmother comfortable.

After making sure his grandmother had everything she needed, he gave her a goodnight kiss on her cheek. "Grandma, there should be plenty of towels in the bathroom. If you need anything, you be sure and let me know, and don't forget, I love you a bushel and a peck." Marlene Frye stood on her tiptoes and hugged her sweet grandson. "You are my sunshine, Mookie Frye."

Mookie left the guestroom and headed back into the kitchen. Upon entering the room, he saw his mom standing by the kitchen table with a piece of paper in her hand. She was reading the handwritten note she found tacked to the back door.

"Well, isn't that so nice." She looked up at Mookie with a smile. "I had asked Butch Baxter to feed the cows for us. Well, he went even farther. He fed all the other animals, filled the water troughs, put fresh hay in the barn, and mowed the lawn around the house. What a great neighbor."

Mookie was relieved that Butch had been so nice to help them while they were out of town for the weekend. He was a great neighbor.

"Oh, wow, that is great, Mom. That helps out a lot." He ran his fingers through his hair and said, "It's been a really long day, Mom. Are you okay? I'm pretty tired, so I'm heading to bed, if that's okay with you. Do you need anything?" Marlene assured Mookie that she was also going to call it a night. "I love you, Mom, and I will see you in the morning." Mookie gave his mom a tight hug and headed down the hallway to his bedroom.

It was hard to put one foot in front of the other as Mookie was overcome with exhaustion. There was a faint squeak as he slowly turned the knob on his bedroom door. Pushing the door open, he bent over and clicked the switch on the lamp by his bed. His heart skipped a beat. On his bedside table was his favorite picture of Stick and Boots. Stick was just a little boy. He was wearing an oversized cowboy hat, with one leg of his jeans tucked haphazardly into one of his cowboy boots, and the other pantleg draping the top of his other one. The two of them were standing in front of the tire bull that Boots had made for Stick. "Tooty Frooty #1." Mookie said as he smiled and took the picture in his hand. He brought it up closer to his face, taking in every single detail of the scene that was captured so many years before. He never realized until that night that his granddad was wearing his "BF" cowboy boots. Suddenly, Mookie was overcome by profound sadness.

"I love you, Dad and I know I never got to meet you, Granddad, but I love you too."

He felt such heaviness in his heart as he gently placed the picture back on the table, got his pajamas on and climbed into bed.

A deep sleep came quickly for the weary teenager. As soon as his head hit the cool, cotton pillowcase that covered his feather pillow, he was out like a light.

In the pitch-black dark of the night, Mookie Frye suddenly sat up in his bed with a jolt. He could have sworn that he heard a commotion. As he got his eyes focused, he saw them. Was he dreaming or was this real?

Standing at the foot of his bed were two apparitions. In a faint glow, flickering like an old silent movie, he saw his dad and his granddad. Stick Frye and Boots Frye were right there at the end of his bed.

At first, they didn't seem to see him or to be present in the room. Mookie rubbed his eyes to get a better look. The two men were right in front of a building that was going up in flames. There was a neon light flashing above their heads, and Mookie could read it as plain as day. It said, "Liquor Store".

The whole thing lasted less than a minute. Mookie couldn't move a muscle. He was transfixed with wonder. It reminded him of Princess Leia's holographic plea for help to Obi Wan Kenobi. They were there, but they were not there. Mookie watched as Stick and Boots turned their backs to him while the building burned to the ground. As the last wall of the building collapsed, the two men slowly turned back around and stared right at Mookie. In one of their hands they each held up a beer can. Next, they pivoted halfway around and looked back at Mookie again. The gesture was foreboding as they lifted their other hands up and pointed to the flashing neon sign. "Liquor Store".

The hair stood up on the back of Mookie's neck. Before they completely disappeared, the gently fading, ghostly figures of Stick and Boots Frye, mouthed the words, "We will never leave you."

His alarm went off, and Mookie Frye's eyes shot wide open.

"Was that real? What did that mean?" He knew he could never tell his mom.

CHAPTER 53

Frosty Allen and the Premise

O ver time, Butch Ed Baxter's heart seemed to harden more and more toward Mookie and Stoney, making it a very tough situation for the two teenagers. School and sporting activities proved to be the hardest of all.

Blackjack Hollow, Oklahoma was a very small town and all three boys loved baseball. Each season had them playing on the same team. "Cooperation" and "teamwork" between them and Butch Ed was a challenge. Adding to the problem, Mookie, Stoney, and Butch Ed were by far the best players on the team. Butch Ed was an amazingly talented third baseman, Mookie's outstanding talents on the mound were making the area papers, and Stoney snagged everything that came his way behind the plate. They were a formidable powerhouse on the field, but as far as Butch Ed was concerned, it was strictly business.

Unfortunately, things got even stickier for the trio. One hot, sultry, summer day, Mookie and Stoney drove to the swimming hole to meet some of their friends. They were all bringing inner tubes to tie together to make a big raft. They planned to push the raft to the middle of the small lake and take turns bouncing on the tubes to jump off into the water.

Mookie's Ford Ranger easily handled the pathway to the pond, and as he set the parking brake to make sure it didn't roll off into the water, he saw a sight that caused him to do a double take.

"No flippin' way." Mookie groaned.

Stoney looked out over the cattails, and across the water. He also groaned. "You've got to be kidding me. What the heck is she thinking?"

Stoney Allen's sister, Frosty, was sitting on a blanket with none other than Butch Ed Baxter. Nothing could be worse than that.

For Stoney, it was hard to see because he knew it would cause him personal grief. For Mookie, it was far worse. Over the summer, Mookie Frye realized he had a secret crush on the prettiest girl in the town, and she was someone near and dear to him. The prettiest girl in town was Frosty Allen. Seeing her with Butch Ed Baxter was devastating.

At that moment, sitting in his pickup, Mookie's heart slipped right out of his chest and shattered in a million pieces.

Furthermore, regardless of Mookie's fervent prayers, Butch Ed Baxter and Frosty Allen continued to go steady for the whole summer.

Stoney reluctantly decided to stay out of his sister's business, and Mookie was determined to hide his true feelings, therefore, seeing Butch Ed and Frosty walking hand in hand down the hall on the first day of school, was brutal.

Frosty would smile and wave at Stoney and Mookie as she strolled by with Butch Ed. She was clueless at their disdain for her choice in a boyfriend. She was also clueless that Mookie Frye was like a lovesick pup.

Mookie would see her at school every day, and each time he hung out with Stoney at the Frye's. He was adamant to not let her know he was hurting inside each time Butch Ed's name was brought up, or worse yet, each time Butch Ed came over when Mookie was there. That was way beyond awkward.

The uneasy situation didn't stop Mookie from teasing Frosty and he didn't let Butch Ed's presence sway him one little bit. In fact, Mookie was positive that he sensed a bit of jealousy from Butch Ed if Frosty showed Mookie any attention at all. For all the grief that Butch Ed had sent Mookie's way, he didn't think it was wrong of him to possibly egg on the jealousy. Deep down inside, Mookie would have been very satisfied if the jealousy reached a fevered pitch. Just a wishful thought, he knew, but it was fun trying anyway.

"Frosty, I would ask you to the prom, but I figure you're already going with that guy," Mookie was sitting at the Allen's kitchen table with Stoney when Butch Ed and Frosty walked through the back door. Mookie squinted up his face as he pointed toward Butch Ed.

"Mookie Frye, you are just shameless! You know I am going with Butch Ed. If you don't have a date yet, I know some of my friends are dying for you to ask them, unless you've already got someone in mind," Frosty smiled and gave Mookie an inquisitive look.

"Oh, Frosty. Wouldn't you like to know? My personal life is such a mystery. I keep all that stuff to myself." Mookie laughed and poked his elbow into Stoney's side. Stoney burst out laughing too.

"Frosty, Mookie and I are probably going stag to the prom. We've talked about it and decided that we would be breaking too many hearts if we narrowed it down to two girls." Stoney, Mookie, and Frosty laughed a hardy laugh. Butch Ed did not.

"Come on, Frosty. Let's leave these two heartthrobs to their chocolate chip cookies and get started on my math. I've got to keep my grades up or I will be in hot water." Butch Ed was the eternal spoilsport when Stoney and Mookie were involved. Frosty let out a sigh, took Butch Ed by the arm and led him into the den where they were going to work on their homework together. In other words, where Frosty would do most of Butch Ed's homework for him. He had honed in on his craft of making himself look like the victim, getting Frosty to feel sorry for him. It worked like a charm every time.

"Frosty, you know I don't like how you look at Mookie. It makes me very uncomfortable. It makes me think that you have some sort of crush on him or something. That would break my heart, Frosty, and you know it." Butch Ed was six -foot-tall, strong-as-an-ox, and as handsome as a Roman gladiator, but he could make himself look like a lost puppy at the snap of a finger.

"Butch Ed, stop that right now. You know Mookie and I have been friends since we were little. He's like a brother to me and you know it. You know you are my guy. I'm going to the prom with you, remember?" Frosty reached over and gave Butch Ed a squeeze to his forearm.

"Let's get busy on our math, Butch Ed. I need to wash my hair tonight, so we've got to get this all done." Frosty put her head back in the math book, and Butch Ed placed his chin in his hand, pouting and staring off into space.

"Okay, how long is Mookie gonna stay here tonight?"

Frosty shot Butch Ed a look and rolled her eyes, then turned back to math.

Even though she was Butch Ed's girlfriend, Frosty did go back and forth in her mind about their relationship. He was good-looking, a star athlete, president of the junior class, and very attentive to her, but it did sometimes get on her nerves the way he constantly needled her about Mookie. She loved Mookie. She loved Mookie like a brother. Didn't she? Weren't her feelings for Mookie like those of two siblings? She reasoned with herself, that she and Mookie were like brother and sister. That was that.

After homework was completed, and Butch Ed was satisfied that Mookie Frye had gone home, he was tenderly pushed out the front door and kindly directed by Frosty to go home too. When the dead bolt on the front door was turned, Frosty headed to the bathroom to wash her hair. As she leaned over the sink, testing the temperature of the water first, she grabbed her bottle of Herbal Essences shampoo and poured a generous amount on the top of her dampened hair. The fresh aroma filled her senses as she scrubbed her head and the lather billowed down into the sink. She followed with the conditioner, all the while her mind kept wandering back to Mookie Frye.

With the towel wrapped around and twisted on top of her head, Frosty Allen looked straight at her reflection in the mirror. She mindlessly reached for her tube of St. Ives apricot blemish cleansing scrub, squeezed out a dollop in her hand, and began to smear it onto her face, never taking her eyes off the mirror.

Mookie Frye was the nicest kid that Frosty had ever known. Actually, he tied with her brother, Stoney, for that honor. Those two boys were peas in a pod and she loved them dearly.

Frosty had never had a class with Mookie until this year. When she moved up from the junior high to the high school, she had one class that was mixed with students from all three grades. There were juniors and seniors in her Sociology class and she and two other girls were the only sophomores. It was after this class each day, when Butch Ed came to walk her to her next class, that he gave her the most flak about Mookie.

"Why do you have to sit by Mookie? You could just as easily sit by a bunch of girls. Every time I walk up you are talking to him. I don't like it, Frosty."

It was beginning to get very old having to listen to Butch Ed harp about Mookie Frye every day. As she stared at her reflection in her bathroom mirror, Frosty told herself that Butch Ed had nothing to worry about. She loved Butch Ed.

However, the moment-of-truth came spilling out as Frosty leaned forward over the sink to rinse the scrub from her face.

When the last particle of the crushed apricot hull scrub was rinsed from her cheeks, she stood directly up and glared at the mirror again. It was written all over her face. Frosty Sue Allen was smitten with Mookie Frye.

She knew by the way she hurried into class to sit in her seat next to his. She knew by the way the butterflies fluttered in her stomach each time he smiled that infectious smile of his. She never missed watching him pitch in a baseball game or ride a bull in the rodeo. Frosty admitted to herself, as she stared at her reflection in the bathroom mirror, that she was in love with Mookie Frye.

"Mookie will never like me in the same way. I need to get over this and just be happy with Butch Ed. Mookie Frye thinks of me like a sister, and I know it."

The sponge rollers were in place in her hair, she was settled in her bed and as she reached over to turn out the lamp on the table beside her bed, she let out a sigh.

"Why can't I stop thinking about Mookie Frye?"

CHAPTER 54:

He's A Suitor

Hannah and Mookie were determined to keep the farm. The work was hard, the hours were long, but come hell or high water, they got it all done.

They had just finished their supper and were sitting around the kitchen table when Hannah brought up the subject of Butch Baxter.

"Mookie, you know we owe such a debt of gratitude to Butch Baxter. He has always been so generous to help us when we need an extra hand. I honestly don't know what we would do without him. He has his own farm to run, but any time we call him, he drops everything and heads over here."

Mookie had been dreading this conversation. He missed his dad tremendously, and he knew that his mom did too. He also knew that his mom was young enough to start over again. He felt nauseous. The thing that made him sick to his stomach was the glaring fact that he didn't want to think about seeing his mom with someone like Butch Baxter.

He couldn't put his finger on why he was uneasy about him. It was just a creepy feeling. He also knew he couldn't deny that his mom was right about Butch Baxter. Butch had gotten them out of so many jams since Stick passed away. He was an excellent cattleman, strong enough to lift anything that needed lifting, savvy enough to recognize a sick cow or calf and smart enough to know exactly what to do to get it well again. None of the help from Butch Baxter had gotten past Mookie. He was very grateful for all of it. However, it also hadn't slipped past Mookie's eyes the way Butch Baxter looked at his mom. Heck, Butch Baxter had been drooling over his mom from the very first day they had all met. Stick used to tease Hannah about Butch and his "googly eyes" any time he was around Hannah. Truth be known, the whole notion of his mom dating Butch Baxter was very unnerving for Mookie. It wasn't the fact that she would be moving on from his dad, it was the whole Butch Ed thing and just bad vibes. Mookie couldn't help but be weirded out by Butch Baxter.

"We do owe him a debt of gratitude, Mom. He seems like a really nice guy." Mookie proceeded with caution. "I guess that's kinda like the code of farmers, isn't it? Helping your neighbors and stuff."

"Yes, Mookie, that is exactly what farmers do for each other. But I believe Butch goes out of his way for us. He's just so sweet and kind." Hannah was twisting her paper napkin around her two fingers as she spoke. She kept looking down at her plate, unable to look Mookie in the eye, "Mookie, he came over today and invited us to go to church with him and Butch Ed. He has been attending a new church just outside of town and has gotten very involved. He is a Wednesday night greeter. Isn't that great, Mookie? I've been wanting us to get back in church. It's just been hard, since your dad and everything. Maybe a new church and a new start is the boost we need. What do you think about that, Mook? I'm also thinking that church would be just the thing to get this problem between you and Butch Ed worked out. Let Jesus take it, ya know?"

It had been a year since the death of his dad and he knew his mom was lonely. He didn't want to stand in the way of her happiness. He also recognized that he was just a kid and what the heck did he know about relationships and adults and gut feelings? He wasn't capable at his young age to be a good judge of Butch Baxter's character. Was he? Maybe or maybe not. He couldn't keep from feeling odd about the whole thing, but he didn't feel like he had the right to stop his mom from pursuing a relationship. His heart ached on a daily basis for Frosty, and he was clueless for a remedy for his dilemma. What the heck did he know?

"Mom, if you want us go to church with Butch, I will give it a try. I can tell you right here and now that I don't have an answer about what to do about Butch Ed. He is the biggest mystery of the century. If you think Jesus can work out this whole thing, I'm game. It won't be easy, I know, but I will try."

"I love you, Mookie. You are such a sweet and precious son. Just like your dad. Sweet and honest as they come." Hannah reached over and gave Mookie's hand a squeeze. "I will call Butch and tell him that we will go with him tomorrow night. I looked at your schedules and you don't have anything on Wednesday night."

His mom looked happy. Mookie's stomach still felt sick, but this was the hand that he and his mom had been dealt.

CHAPTER 55:

They Went Churchin'

"Welcome to The Church of Jubilation. Rejoice! We Can't Contain our Great Happiness!" Mookie peered at the sign proudly displayed at the entry to the vast parking lot in front of the mall-looking building.

"Mom, is this the church? I don't see any crosses." Mookie spoke up from the back seat of Butch Baxter's pickup truck. Butch Ed had refused to ride with them, insisting on driving his own car to church. That didn't bother Mookie in the least. He could think of better things to occupy his time on a ten-mile trip than being confined in the back seat with Butch Ed Baxter. Fun things, like thinking about Frosty Allen.

Hannah was in the front seat with Butch. She was also rubber-necking as they drove into the parking lot.

"Butch, I guess that's my question too. Our little Methodist church has a prominent cross on its steeple. I see this church doesn't have a steeple either…" Her voice trailed off as Butch pulled the vehicle into a convenient parking space.

After he put the truck in park and switched off the engine, Butch Baxter turned to face Hannah and Mookie, "I can understand your concerns. This church is trying to be welcoming to all who seek Jesus. To some people, religious displays are kinda overwhelming. I guess, just keep an open mind. I will say for myself, this place has brought me closer to the Lord than I've ever been in my life and now I understand what being saved by the blood of Jesus is all about."

With that said, the three of them got out of Butch's truck and went inside the church.

Hannah and Mookie were in awe as they watched Butch Baxter during the praise and worship service. The music was uplifting and, well, jubilant. They saw him raise his hand up to the sky, his eyes were closed, and his brow was furrowed. Shouts of "Thank you, Jesus!" sprang from his lips, as he clapped and clicked his heels at the conclusion of the final song.

Later that evening, back home at their farm, Hannah and Mookie were sitting at the kitchen table, with their hands cupped around their mugs of hot chocolate.

"What did you think about the church tonight, Mookie?" Hannah looked up from watching the steam rise from her hot chocolate.

"It was fine, Mom. Lots of nice people, and I totally got what the pastor meant in his message." Mookie hesitated, then took a deep breath, "Mom, my question to you is, what do you think about Butch? That's a different side of him than I've ever seen. Do you think all that was real?" Mookie tilted his chin down and looked right at his mom.

"What do you mean, son? Real? Are you saying that you think Butch might have been putting on an act? How can you say something like that? I'm surprised to hear those words come out of your mouth, Mookie Frye. You've never been judgmental in the least, and I don't want you to start being that way now. Of all things!" Hannah immediately rose from the table and took her mug of hot chocolate over to the sink, keeping her back to Mookie.

"I'm sorry, Mom. Really. I am. I don't mean to be judging anyone. Maybe I just don't know him that well. Please, Mom. I'm sorry." Mookie apologized profusely to his mother. Sitting in silence at the kitchen table, staring at Hannah's back, Mookie realized, then and there, that he and his mom were entering a strange new phase of their relationship. Even though he was only seventeen-years-old, Mookie knew that he was going to have to tread lightly when it came to Butch Baxter.

"Mookie, I want you to give Butch a chance here. I don't know where this is going either, but I do know that he's very nice to me. To us. He's helpful and kind. Just help me out and try not to judge him before you get to know him. I miss your dad too, but I also realize that I would like to be part of a couple again. I miss that. I miss that a lot."

If only he had someone to talk to about all of this. What was the sick feeling in his stomach all about when it came to Butch Baxter? Was he jealous of Butch? Was that it? Mookie's main concern was his mom's well-being and happiness. If Butch Baxter was the man to take her loneliness away and make her happy, he could deal with that – he wanted the best for his mom. Or was it something else? He really needed someone to talk to about his mom and Butch Baxter.

Mookie pushed himself away and stood up from the table. After pausing for a moment, he walked over to the sink, gave his mom a hug, and told her goodnight.

The short walk down the hallway to his bedroom seemed to take longer than usual on this particular night. Stepping into the moonlit area in front of his bedroom window, he could see there was a light breeze that had the curtain billowing gently. Mookie was glad to be in his room. He felt safe and comforted. Since his father's death, his bedroom had become his refuge, his shelter in the storm.

His mom was falling in love with Butch Baxter. He knew it. Standing alone in the quiet of his room, staring out the window at the shadows of the night, Mookie heard a coyote howl a sad and eerie cry. He couldn't hold back and decided to join in with the lonesome, shape-shifting canine, as the tears began to fall.

Mookie Frye missed his dad so much it hurt.

CHAPTER 56:

Mookie Frye for Class President

At the beginning of their senior year, Mookie Frye decided to throw his hat in the ring and run for Senior Class President. The shoe-in victor up until that point had been the inevitable leader of the senior class, Butch Ed Baxter. Butch Ed Baxter had been the president of every one of his classes since the seventh grade. He always ran, and he always won. He had never even been challenged. Not once had another name been on the same ballot as Butch Ed Baxter's. That is, not until Mookie Frye walked into the high school office and requested the form.

"Good morning, Mrs. Hoffman, I would like to have the form to fill out to run for class office. They're due today, aren't they?"

Mrs. Hoffman, the principal's secretary, looked across the counter at Mookie as she walked toward the stack of papers on the credenza. The forms for running for a class office.

"They certainly are due today. Before school is out this afternoon, and not a minute later. Which one do you want, Mookie? Vice-President? Secretary-Treasurer? Executive Board?"

"Mrs. Hoffman, I will take the blue one there in that stack. The one for Senior Class President."

Mrs. Hoffman's jaw dropped open as she looked at Mookie over her half-glasses.

"You are going to run for Senior Class President, Mookie? You do realize that Butch Ed Baxter has already turned his form in for that position." Mrs. Hoffman licked her pointer finger and pulled down on the corner of the yellow sheet from its place in the stack. The yellow sheet was the form for running for Senior Class Vice-President.

"The blue one, Mrs. Hoffman. I will take the blue one. Senior Class President. I think I will go ahead and fill it out while I'm here. I don't want to miss the deadline." Mookie donned a crooked smile as Mrs. Hoffman slowly slid the blue form into his waiting hand.

It was going to be an epic battle.

CHAPTER 57:

The Benevolent Butch Baxter

Mookie wasn't sure how to react. He was in such a state of confusion where Butch Baxter was concerned, he didn't know whether to be happy or worried. He was fully aware that a lot of cool things come with the teenage years, but unfortunately, wisdom isn't always as appreciated as a driver's license or unaccompanied admission to adult rated movies. For the life of him, he just couldn't nail down the cause of the intense anxiety that gripped his stomach at the very mention of the name, Butch Baxter.

Multi-colored fall leaves were skipping across the yard as Mookie slowly drove his truck onto the concrete portion of their driveway. Off to the side, parked by the gnarly blackjack oak tree, was a brand spanking new John Deere, fully enclosed cab tractor, adorned with a huge red bow.

Hannah was jumping up and down with glee, Butch Baxter had a grin on his face a mile-wide, and Mookie was having a hard time remembering to put his truck in park.

Dumbstruck. That was his reaction. Just plain old dumbstruck.

When Mookie was finally able to be jarred back to his senses enough to get out of his truck, Hannah ran over to him with tears of joy streaming down her face.

"Mookie, can you believe this? Come over here, Butch. I want you to stand here with us. Mookie, Butch has something to say to you." Hannah wrapped one arm around Mookie's waist, and motioned to Butch with the other.

Butch Baxter asked Hannah if it would be okay if they moved the conversation over to the front porch, where they could sit down and talk. Hannah quickly agreed.

Hannah and Butch sat side-by-side on the porch swing. Mookie chose the bright red wooden rocking chair, with the multi-colored horse blanket seat cushion. It had been his dad, Stick's, favorite chair. Somehow Mookie sensed he would need leverage in the looming conversation and being perched in Stick's chair seemed fitting.

Butch Baxter reached over, took Hannah's hand in his, and gave it a gentle squeeze.

"Mookie, I want you to know, right here and now, that I think the world of you and your beautiful mother. In fact, I'm mighty proud to say, I have fallen deeply in love with this precious lady sitting here by my side. I assure you that I will see to it she will be taken care of the rest of her life."

Hannah's face blushed a rosy pink. Butch continued, "That tractor sitting out there in the yard is just a small token of my love. This, is a token of my undying devotion." Butch Baxter arose from the porch swing like a pompous statesman, chivalrously taking Hannah's hands in his. The fluid motion was gentle as he lifted her from her seat. As she drew near him, he reached into the back pocket of his jeans, pulled out a small black box, and knelt down on one knee.

Mookie's immediate instinct prodded him to run straight at the interloper and knock him over before the outcome of this grand gesture was sealed by a kiss. A very insistent voice inside his head was loudly pleading with his mother, "Please don't say yes, Mom!"

"Hannah Frye, will you marry me?"

The kiss sealed the deal, and Hannah and Butch encircled each other in a warm embrace. Mookie's grip on the chair arms tightened as he faked a congratulatory smile. His head was spinning, and his stomach was tied in a multitude of knots while he contemplated the outcome, fallout, and ramifications of his mother's decision to marry Butch Baxter. No matter which angle he approached it, the bottom line for Mookie was the stark realization that if his mother marries Butch, Mookie's life going forward was gonna suck.

"God, please help me get a grip on this situation. Dad, are you out there? Can you please help me?" Mookie's thoughts raced. Hannah and Butch were talking to him, but he found it impossible to focus. He nodded his head and smiled, hoping against hope, that they would be momentarily appeased while he tried to catch himself from falling into the abyss.

He was the son, and she was the mother. Cold, hard facts of life. Mookie rammed his hands deep in his jeans pockets with his left hand securely gripping the keys to his truck. If only he could jump in his Ford Ranger, put the key in the ignition, and drive away. He just wanted to drive away.

Later that afternoon, after Butch went home, Mookie was wrapping up his chores when he had the sudden urge to go in the house to find his mother. He quickly discovered her sitting in the den, crocheting an afghan.

Still holding a water pail in his hand, he matter-of-factly said to his mother, "Mom, I want you to be happy. If Butch Baxter is the guy to make that happen, I'm in your corner."

He spun around and went back out to the barnyard. That was that.

CHAPTER 58:

The Campaign Heats Up

When Butch Ed Baxter heard that Mookie Frye was running against him for Senior Class President, he almost rammed his fist through his locker door.

"That punk! That freakin' punk! This is war. All-out war." Butch Ed's jaw was set. The battle was looming.

Stoney Allen decided to run for Senior Class Vice-President, therefore it made perfect sense that Mookie and Stoney would help each other with their campaigns.

Their first campaign organizing meeting was held in the Frye's hay loft. Stoney and Mookie had settled comfortably into two piles of soft alfalfa hay. Stoney was sipping on a Grape Nehi soda, Mookie's choice was Orange Crush. His dad's favorite.

"We've got to have Star Wars themes." Stoney stated, as he swigged the last drops from his bottle of pop.

"Absolutely. It's most definitely got to be Star Wars." They both laughed at their total lack of shame at being such nerds.

"So, okay, let's think of our campaign slogans. You go first, Stoney."

Stoney sat for a moment, deep in thought, rolling the empty soda pop bottle between his two hands, "I've got one for Butch Ed." He flashed a sly grin at Mookie.

"Lay it on me."

Stoney pushed the bill of his baseball cap upwards a bit and looked at his fellow candidate.

"Help me, Obi-Wan Kenobi. You're my only hope."

Mookie laughed so hard, he almost spewed out his orange pop.

After their very productive organizational meeting in the barn, Stoney and Mookie settled on their game plans and strategies. They were also quite satisfied with the slogans they had chosen.

Stoney Allen was sure to be the next class vice-president with his choice. It was a quote from Yoda, "Do. Or do not. There is no try."

Mookie felt like he hit it out of the ballpark with his slogan. He could see it already. He would make posters and put them up all around the school. Thank you, Luke Skywalker.

Mookie Frye for Senior Class President. "I'm a Jedi like my father before me." It was pure brilliance.

CHAPTER 59

The New Class President Is...

It had been a boisterous campaign from Butch Ed Baxter's front line. His loyal disciples demonstrated an amazing effort of fine-tuned organizational skills. Or, probably closer to the truth, it was mostly due to the fact that Butch Ed bribed, charmed, and wheedled the high school varsity cheerleaders to help him in his election efforts. Hence, the entire two weeks of the campaign, the girls flashed their "Vote for Butch Ed" cheer in the hallways every morning before school. With their pom-poms poised at their hips, they pranced, danced, and wiggled to Butch Ed's self-penned chant.

"Butch Ed Baxter is the best! He is better than the rest! Don't be kookie and vote for Mookie. Butch Ed Baxter is the Best!"

However corny Butch Ed's manipulations may have seemed, things were looking very promising for a victorious conclusion, for the simple reason that Mookie Frye was running a very low-key campaign. Low-key was actually putting it mildly. Mookie's campaign production was down-right humdrum. The chatter in the classrooms leaned toward the realization that a vote for Mookie Frye could possibly be a wasted checkmark toward a lackluster senior year.

For every ditsy blonde cheerleader passing out Dum Dum suckers with Butch Ed's campaign slogan secured to the stick with a piece of pipe cleaner, it was pretty much crickets from Mookie's side of the aisle.

"Hey, Janie, here's a Butch Ed sucker. Remember to vote for him on Friday. Read the slogan too. It is so cute!" She was a blonde cheerleader named Misty.

"Take a Butch Ed sucker, Jack. See the slogan? It says, 'Vote for Butch Ed – You Won't Be Misled.' Isn't that so clever? Vote for Butch Ed Baxter on Friday!" She was a blonde cheerleader named Becky.

Mookie Frye had plastered the hallways with his posters and had taped one on each side of his pickup truck bed. Beyond that, when he wasn't in class, he could be found in the high school gym lifting weights. Butch Ed Baxter was everywhere, smiling, passing out Dum Dum suckers, and pressing his fellow classmates for their votes.

The student body of Blackjack Hollow High School had been instructed to assemble in the gymnasium for the crescendo at ten o'clock Friday morning. The campaign period was over, and all candidates had one last chance to sway votes with their speeches to the electorate. After the assembly, the marked ballots were to be deposited in the ballot boxes that had been placed at the gym exit.

It was a blustery fall morning in Blackjack Hollow. Hannah and Mookie sat at the kitchen table, chatting over breakfast. As had become custom of late, the conversation was mundane, leaning more toward the weather, farming, and the weather. The elephant in the room loomed larger than ever.

Hannah brought it up first. "Mookie, are you going to be okay if you lose the election to Butch Ed? I know we haven't talked about it much. I've kinda struggled on the best way to talk about it with you. You and I both know it's an uncomfortable subject. Butch seems to think that maybe you two are just going through male turf wars or whatever that's called. Like a growing up process. He's worried that it will make things worse between you and Butch Ed, if Butch Ed wins. It's just so sad, you two used to be such good friends. I guess what I'm trying to say is, this is all very overwhelming for both of us, son. I've been reading about blending families and there's going to be challenges. I just wish..."

"Mom. Stop. Please, just stop. I don't want to get into any of that this morning. I must say, your confidence in me is underwhelming. You can just tell that Butch Baxter that maybe he needs to worry about Butch Ed's feelings if he loses. Jeez, Mom. Trust me, whatever happens today, I will be just fine."

"Okay, Mookie. I'm sorry. You're right, today is not a day for that stuff. Today is a great day. I am going to be the mother of a president!"

"I wouldn't have run if I didn't think I could win. I'm a Jedi, remember? The Force is with me. See you after school, Mom." He pointed up toward heaven, gave her a big hug, and headed outside to drive to school.

Mookie parked his pickup in his regular parking spot in the high school parking lot. The stack of books from homework was sitting in the passenger side. Before getting out of his vehicle, he leaned over them to open his glove compartment, just like he did every morning.

When the door to the compartment came forward, Mookie pulled out the picture of Frosty. That's how he started each school day. Looking at her picture.

This morning, he needed to look at her picture more than ever. "Frosty Sue Allen, looking at you gives me hope." He kissed the glossy paper, put her image back in the glove compartment, and pushed the door until it clicked.

Stoney Allen was waiting for him at the entrance to the school.

"Good morning, Mr. President-to-be," Stoney smiled at Mookie as he held the door open for his friend.

"You look very vice-presidential this morning, Stoney. Let's go get this show on the road."

Mrs. Hoffman was putting push pins in the corners of a sheet of paper on the school bulletin board when Mookie and Stoney walked up to her.

"Excuse me, Mrs. Hoffman. Is that the program for the assembly this morning?" Mookie was pointing to the sheet of paper on the bulletin board.

Mrs. Hoffman looked over her shoulder at Mookie and replied, "Why, yes, it is, Mookie. Looks like you got the luck of the draw. You are set to speak last."

Mookie was thrilled. Things were going exactly as he had planned them.

"May I have your attention, students? We will stand and say the Pledge of Allegiance before we get this assembly underway." Mr. Allen, the high school principal, placed his right hand on his heart, and led the student body in the pledge.

Some of the speeches garnered more laughs than votes. Many others were superfluous, boring and quite obviously written by their parents. Coming as no surprise to anyone, Stoney's speech knocked it out of the ballpark, and Mookie had no doubt that his best friend would be the next senior class vice-president, hands-down.

Butch Ed Baxter was feeling extremely confident going into the final day of the campaign. He had amassed more than an ample number of promises from classmates that they were casting their votes for him. Therefore, he wasn't the least bit nervous when Mr. Allen called his name to come to the podium to give his speech.

"Thank you, Mr. Allen, and thank you to the entire senior class for giving me the opportunity to speak to you today. As you all know, I have been the president of our class since the seventh grade. I am the only one on this stage today that can say they have leadership experience. I've done a great job in the past and I know I can continue to do a great job our final year in this wonderful school. Leadership is about mapping out where you need to go to win as a team. My opponent says he is a Jedi. I say I am a leader. Please mark your ballot for Butch Ed Baxter, for Senior Class President."

The majority of the senior class gave Butch Ed Baxter a deafening round of applause. Butch Ed stepped away from the podium and returned to his seat on the dais, feeling quite smug.

"Thank you, Butch Ed. Now, to wrap things up, I would like to call Mookie Frye to the podium to give his speech." Mr. Allen motioned to Mookie to come to the microphone.

Mookie ambled over to the podium. Butch Ed Baxter had worn a suit and tie to school today, and Mookie stood in stark contrast in his western shirt and Wrangler jeans. Butch Ed had spoken with grit and confidence. Mookie started out his speech with humility, his cheeks flushing bright red.

"Thanks, everyone. I'm glad to be able to be up here. I wanna start off by sayin', Butch Ed just gave a great speech. There's no doubt about that, and he has been a great leader since the seventh grade. And, yeah, I did say I was a Jedi. Ya know, I just love Star Wars. I love the theme of the movie. It's the underdogs fighting for those that can't fight for themselves, against some really bad people. The Jedi study and utilize the Force, in order to help and protect those in need. I really don't want to be a leader, I just want to be a fighter. Fight for what's right. To protect people. My dad was my hero. He was, and I guess he still is, my Force. He loved helping people. So, if you vote for me, I promise we can do something together this year to help others. This is our senior year. Let's leave something behind that is charitable and kind. Thank you."

He won by a landslide.

CHAPTER 60:

Mookie Takes a Stand

It was homecoming at Blackjack Hollow High School. Blackjack Hollow's football team was slated to play Oologah, their big rival, with the kickoff set for eight o'clock that evening. Mookie and Stoney had commandeered the construction of the float entered by the senior class. They got outvoted for a Star Wars theme but were happy to lend their creative talents when the committee picked a football theme instead.

The parade went off without a hitch, one of Mookie's best friends since grade school, Piper Landers, was elected homecoming queen, and Blackjack Hollow romped Oologah 28-6.

Stoney and Mookie decided against going to the homecoming dance. Stoney didn't like to dance, and Mookie's secret crush on Frosty kept him from putting undue angst on himself by watching Butch Ed Baxter hold her in his arms on the dance floor.

Mookie and Stoney made plans to hang out the next day, said goodbye, and headed home.

Hannah was in bed asleep when Mookie got home from the football game. He fixed himself a bologna and crushed potato chip sandwich and settled in the den to watch USA Up All Night until he got sleepy or at least until he could get his mind off Frosty dancing the night away with Butch Ed Baxter. Thankfully, sleepiness set in first and he was off to bed.

Mookie's bedroom door opened, and he could see his mom standing in the glow from the kitchen light. He never heard the phone ring. The clock on his bedside table displayed two o'clock in the morning.

"Mook, Mookie, wake up, sweetie."

"Yeah, Mom, okay, what's wrong?" He ran his fingers through his hair and sat up on the side of his bed. His mom came and sat down beside him.

"Mookie, I have some terrible news." Mookie immediately put his head in his hands.

"What is it, Mom? Just tell me it's not Grandma. Please tell me Grandma is okay."

"Yes, Mookie, your Grandma is just fine. Honey, I just got off the phone with Stoney's dad. It seems that after the dance last night a bunch of kids drove out to the bluffs for a big party. There was a lot of alcohol."

"Oh my God, Mom. What happened?" Mookie had a look of sheer terror on his face.

"There was a head-on collision. Brad Johnson and Piper Landers. I'm so sorry, Mookie. Brad was drunk and ran into another car head-on. There are terrible injuries, Mookie, and I'm sorry to tell you that Piper didn't make it. She died instantly."

Hannah was unable to console Mookie. He kept crying out until he lost his voice completely, "I hate alcohol! I hate alcohol! Not Piper! Not Piper!"

Mookie couldn't believe the horrible news his mother had just told him about one of his dearest friends. Piper was gone and he was devastated.

Her funeral was held in the high school gymnasium. Piper's parents asked Mookie to give the eulogy.

"Piper Landers was my friend since first grade. She was the happiest person I have ever known. I don't know what was bigger, her love for her dog, Zippy, or her smile. Maybe it was a tie. Yeah, I'm sure it was a tie," Mookie took a deep breath and continued, "It's hard to stand here and talk about her in the past tense. I still can't believe she is gone. Hang on a minute." Mookie wiped his tears onto his shirtsleeve. "Ya know it's hard to talk about her and not cry. We all loved Piper and now she is gone. Our sweet Piper Landers is gone and there's only one reason. She's gone because a choice was made to get behind the steering wheel of a car and drive drunk. Period. Alcohol killed our friend, Piper. That's why I'm standing here right now. Piper's mom and dad asked me to talk today so that's what I'm doin'. As of Monday, we are forming a Blackjack Hollow High School chapter of Students Against Drunk Driving. We are going to name it The Piper Landers Chapter of Students Against Drunk Driving. Mr. and Mrs. Landers, I promise you that our chapter of this organization will do great things in your daughter's name. We will do whatever we can to see that a tragedy like this doesn't ever happen again." Mookie lowered his head for a moment, then looked up toward heaven, "We will miss you, Piper. Your death will not be vain, I promise you that."

CHAPTER 61

Butch Baxter and the Pheasant Hunting Trip

Mookie was holed up in his bedroom. The conversation between Butch Baxter and Hannah Frye was making him extremely uncomfortable. He sat on his bed tossing a baseball up and down, catching it in his glove. He could only hear bits and pieces of the conversation, and unfortunately for Mookie, the one thing he did hear was his mom telling Butch that she did love him. That part made him sick. If it were up to him, he would storm out of his room and tell that lumbering doofus standing in his mom's kitchen to take a one-way trip on a slow boat to China. Sadly, Mookie knew he needed to stay out of it, and truthfully, it wasn't really a fight. It was more of a whining fest on Butch's part. Now Mookie knew where Butch Ed got his whining and nuts don't fall too far from the tree.

Butch was frustrated at Hannah because she wouldn't commit to a wedding date. Mookie heard something about next spring, and then after a few seconds of mumbling from Butch, Mookie heard Butch start his truck, followed by the sound of gravel crunching as he drove away.

He heard his mom's footsteps coming down the hall. Hannah stuck her head in Mookie's bedroom and in her most cheerful voice said, "Hey, Mookie, do you want some popcorn? Doogie Howser is on and I thought we might watch it together."

"Mom, where in the world did you get that I like to watch Doogie Howser? That show is so lame. Star Trek is on though. I'll watch that with you, and please put lots of butter on the popcorn." It did not surprise Mookie one bit that his mother acted as if nothing was wrong. If she wasn't going to bring up Butch Baxter, it was a good day for Mookie.

"Oh, and Mook, Butch is taking a pheasant hunting trip in November. He's going with some of his friends, and he was planning to invite his dad and Butch Ed. He also wanted me to see if you wanted to go too." Hannah was giving Mookie one of her "it won't hurt you to do this one thing just for me" looks.

"Mom. Mom. Why are you doing this to me? If you want Butch Baxter in your life, that is 100% your business. Just because you chose him doesn't mean that it's a package deal with Butch Ed. I can't stand Butch Ed Baxter. He has dealt me so much misery. I'm tellin' you, Mom, it's not gonna work between Butch Ed and me and you can't make me think anything different. You are living in a dream world and your dream is becoming my nightmare."

"I guess that means you are going to pass on the hunting trip?" Mookie was incredulous at his mother's persistence, but one thing he knew about Hannah Frye, she never backed down from a challenge.

Furthermore, neither did he. Butch Baxter's hunting trip went forward as planned, and much to Hannah's chagrin, Mookie Frye stayed home.

CHAPTER 62:

Big League Chew, Baseball, and Bound for State

It was a harsh winter around Blackjack Hollow, Oklahoma that year, and Mookie got extremely tired of being indoors. For that reason, the first sunny day in spring found Mookie Frye and the Blackjack Hollow High School varsity baseball team out on the practice field, anxious for the start of the season. They were the defending 2A state champs for the last two years and were champing at the bit to grab the title again. Especially, Mookie, Stoney, Butch Ed, and the other graduating seniors, as they wanted to put one last trophy front and center in the high school trophy case.

Consequently, a few short weeks into the season, they were well on their way to making that dream a reality.

With his signature wad of Big League Chew crammed in his mouth, Mookie took to the mound time after time sending batter after batter back to the bench. Blackjack Hollow was clobbering their opponents. Standing them up and setting them down – hard.

Blackjack Hollow High School was undefeated and headed for the state championship game.

CHAPTER 63:

The Kiss

As Mookie had promised Piper Landers' parents, the Piper Landers Chapter of Students Against Drunk Driving, was set to do great things. The whole premise behind the organization was that it was to be peer led. SADD's approach involved young people presenting education and preventative messages through school and community activities to get the word out that drinking and driving is a destructive decision. Kids talking to other kids in their own language, hopefully persuading them to think twice about making the stupid and, often times, fatal decision to drink and drive.

Mookie Frye had been known for several years to be a staunch fighter against alcohol, therefore, becoming the leader of the local chapter of Students Against Drunk Driving, was par for the course for him. Everyone in Blackjack Hollow knew he would take his role quite seriously.

Mookie Frye and Stoney Allen headed up a SADD fundraiser for the following Saturday in downtown Blackjack Hollow. The flourishing chapter had been selling raffle tickets for a month. The entire community was enthusiastically on board, and several area businesses had donated prizes for the raffle. The local VFW, thanks to Mookie's good friend, Charley Bowman, was gearing up to hold a pancake breakfast that morning with all proceeds going to SADD.

Additionally, the owner of the local salvage yard had donated an old car for the fundraising efforts. It was just the shell of a vehicle, with no motor, so he hauled it over to the town square for the SADD members, where they were going to set up a Car Bash. Each person could take a sledge hammer to the car, three bashes for one dollar.

Apparently, there was a lot of pent up aggression in that town, as the line for the Car Bash circled around the corner and the proceeds went through the roof.

Mookie's first event, in his dear friend Piper's honor, was a tremendous success.

"Stoney, we made over a thousand dollars! Can you believe it? This is so great. This will help us buy pamphlets to hand out at all the places where kids hang out. School dances, sporting events and stuff. I can even take some with me to the rodeos." Mookie and Stoney gave each other high fives, and were putting the proceeds in the bank bag when they saw the reflection of headlights sweep across the building wall.

It was Frosty.

"I wanted to come by and congratulate you guys for the wonderful fundraiser. I know how hard you both worked on this thing and I couldn't be prouder of a couple of guys than I am of you two right now."

They both walked over to Frosty and gave her simultaneous hugs.

"Thank you, Little Bit." That was Stoney's pet name for his younger sister.

"Yeah, thanks, Frosty. That means a lot, coming from you and everything." Mookie surprised himself. Seeing Frosty in the headlights of her car made him feel a little weak inside. He was glad it was dark. He knew that his face was turning a hundred shades of red.

"Hey, Mookie, can you stay here with Frosty for a minute? I'm gonna run to catch my dad over there before he drives off and give him this money for safe keeping. I'll be right back, and we can all go over to the Rocket and get a coke." Stoney was gone in a flash, leaving Mookie and Frosty standing together by her car.

Mookie Frye had never felt this awkward around Frosty Sue Allen in his life. His mind went totally blank as he stood facing her. He could feel the tops of his ears burning hot and sweat was pooling in the palms of his hands. Frosty looked up at him with a slight grin, and before he knew it, she was on her tiptoes planting a sweet kiss on his lips. He grabbed her by the elbows, bringing her in closer to him. He didn't ever want the kiss to end.

"Frosty! I knew it! You and Mookie. I just knew it."

Butch Ed Baxter walked up behind Frosty. Just in time to see the kiss.

CHAPTER 64:

Butch Ed Baxter Is a Sore Loser

The state championship game was four days away. Practices were becoming brutal for Mookie. Not because they were exhausting or intense, they were becoming unbearable for Mookie because he stole Butch Ed's girl from him right under Butch Ed's nose. That's not exactly how it happened, but from Butch Ed's hopping mad perspective, Mookie Frye deserved to be destroyed and Butch Ed Baxter was just the man for the job.

Butch Ed was determined to sabotage Mookie's efforts on the mound in any way, shape or form, that he could contrive. Oopsies from his third base position, whereby a missile, disguised as a baseball, barely missed Mookie's glove, striking him directly in the hip, shin, or "other" area. "Accidental" collisions on the infield if Mookie signaled that he had the pop fly, and Butch Ed "innocently" missed Mookie's call.

The coaches seemed oblivious to Butch Ed's antics, marking them up as pre-championship jitters on both Butch Ed's and Mookie's part.

After Wednesday afternoon's practice, Coach Pierce gathered the team together in the dugout.

"Guys, I know we have been showing a little bit of discombobulation in our practices, and I am fully aware that all of the rain we've been having this week hasn't helped either. Believe me, I've been there, and Coach Grigsby, and Coach Smith, have both been there too. It's okay to be nervous going into a championship game like we are facing on Friday. We've got this, guys. You know it and I know it. Today's practice is our last before the game. We're not going to have practice tomorrow, so I want you all to take a day to rest and get focused. Just keep your eye on the tiger, your nerves steady, and we're gonna come together as the undefeated team that we know we are. Now listen up, the bus will be leaving here Friday morning at nine. Get a good breakfast and be here no later than eight-thirty. We play at one o'clock on Tulsa Memorial High School's field. We will have a light lunch before the game and the booster club has informed me that they will be waiting for us for dinner at Casa Bonita, to celebrate our win. Now let's go home."

Mookie and Butch Ed were standing side-by-side as they shoved their bats and gloves into their duffle bags.

As he yanked on the string to close his bag, Butch Ed leaned into Mookie and whispered in his ear, "Mookie Frye, if you're wondering, I don't give a rat's behind about winning the game. My goal is to make you look like a laughingstock. No one will want to recruit you when I'm done. See you Friday, punk."

CHAPTER 65:

Hannah at the Hardware Store

Thursday morning, before Mookie left for school, he asked his mom if she would mind going into town and getting him a couple of bottles of Gatorade for the game the next day. The rain in the northeastern parts of Oklahoma had finally stopped, leaving the air sultry and humid. Gatorade would help Mookie stay hydrated while he pitched.

"I sure will. Do you need anything else while I'm in town? Are you set with enough Big League Chew?" Hannah smiled at her son as he stood in the doorway.

"Yep, I'm good there. I'm just halfway through the last box we got from Mr. Hollister. He sure is a nice guy. Oh, and I almost forgot, while you're in town, you might want to go to the hardware store and buy a door latch. The one on the chicken coop finally rusted in half." Mookie said as he pulled his truck keys out of the front pocket of his jeans.

231

"Yes, that's right. Thanks for reminding me, honey. Oh, and before you go, will you be home for supper tonight? I could cook something special for you to have a good home-cooked meal. Butch said something about taking me out for pizza, but I already told him that you are my priority tonight." Hannah came over to the doorway to give her son a hug.

"No, that's okay, Mom. Go ahead with the pizza date with Butch. I'm going to hang out with some of the guys over at Stoney's for most of the evening. We've got some strategizing to do." As Mookie turned to walk to his truck, Hannah winked and said one last thing to him, "Say hello to Frosty for me, Mookie."

Mookie blushed and waved goodbye to his mom.

After Hannah jotted a few other items down on her list of things she needed from town, she grabbed her purse and headed out the door.

She bought Mookie's Gatorade, and a few more groceries at the Humpty Dumpty, some crocheting thread at Mary Jane's Fabric Store, and stopped in the feed store for a block of salt for the cows. When she had the grocery sacks and the salt block secured in the back seat of her pickup truck, Hannah pulled her list from her purse and saw that the last item left was the door latch at the hardware store.

Hannah walked across the street to go into the store, never noticing Butch Baxter's truck parked directly in front of the entrance.

Just as she was getting ready to ask for help in locating the correct size door latch for her chicken coop, she spotted a small box of them on a bottom shelf. When she leaned down to pick one out, she peered through the shelving and saw the legs of three men as they stood together talking in the next aisle. She immediately recognized one set of legs to be those of her fiancé, Butch Baxter.

Their hushed exchanges and earthy chuckles were being kept low. Therefore, overcome by curiosity, Hannah got on her knees and stuck her head halfway through the shelving, close enough to hear everything they were saying.

Hannah was livid. She wasted no time in pulling herself out of the bottom shelf and jumping to her feet. Her hand was gripped tightly around the handle of her purse and it was all she could do to contain her fury. Marching toward the checkout, she quickly paid for her door latch and hurried out the door.

The one thing Hannah Frye knew, and knew without a doubt, she was going to waylay Butch Baxter when he stepped his good-for-nothing foot in her house tonight.

CHAPTER 66:

The Confrontational Blow

The telephone on the wall in Hannah's kitchen rang loudly and furiously. It was probably Butch, and Hannah was having a hard time placing her hand on the receiver to pick it up. She needed to collect her thoughts on the best way to handle the situation, concluding instinctively that it was a monumental relief that Mookie was over at Stoney Allen's house. Mookie would blow a gasket if he knew what Hannah found out about Butch. Therefore, Hannah figured it was best that she would handle it and tell Mookie the story after it was over, and Butch was long gone.

"Hello." Hannah tried to act as normally as she could.

"Hi, Baby. You sound kinda quiet. Are you okay? I'm calling to see if you were going to cook for Mookie or go to eat pizza with me." Butch was his usual sappy self.

"I'm just fine, Butch. I'm sorta in a hurry though, I was just walking out the door to feed the horses. They've already seen me, so I don't want them to get all antsy. How about you come over here at six. Will that work?"

"Sure, it will, but…" Butch wasn't wanting to let Hannah off the phone so fast.

She interrupted him mid-sentence, "Great, see you at six."

Hannah hung up the phone, brandishing a smirk. The horses had been fed two hours ago.

At six o'clock sharp, Hannah saw Butch Baxter's truck pull into her driveway. As she peeked out the window curtains, she noticed he was carrying a bouquet of roses.

"Big, fat, hairy deal, Butch Baxter. You can keep your nasty flowers." Hannah whispered to herself as she watched Butch walk up the steps to her front door.

She didn't even wait for him to knock when she jerked the door open.

He knew immediately that Hannah Frye was mad.

As promised, Hannah waylaid Butch Baxter right in the foyer of her living room.

She didn't let him get a word in edge-wise at first. Hannah relayed to him the fact that she overheard his conversation in the aisle of the hardware store.

Apparently, when Butch, his father, his friends, and Butch Ed went to Kansas on the pheasant hunting trip, they made an excursion outside of Salina, Kansas, to a gentlemen's club with strip-tease dancers, called *The Wild Wild West*. Butch had laughed bodaciously as he told his friends in the hardware store how he and his fellow hunters had frequented the strip club every year since he and his dad had been going to Kansas on their hunting trips. He bragged without shame that he paid for a "rite of passage lap dance" for his eighteen-year-old son, Butch Ed. Hannah emphatically expressed to Butch her horror as she relayed how she overheard him using the most vulgar language to describe every detail of the establishment and the dancers.

"Mookie, was right. You were putting on an act at the church. You have been putting on an act the whole time with me. I should have listened to my son. You make me sick, Butch Baxter." Hannah's hands were clenched at her sides as she stood toe-to-toe with him.

Unfortunately for Hannah, Butch Baxter had most definitely been putting on an act in front of Hannah. He was an imposter, and she was just about to discover the extent of what kind of evil was hidden behind his "good-old-boy" mask.

Butch hurled the bouquet of roses so hard they knocked over a lamp on the nearby table. He rushed toward Hannah and grabbed her arm before she realized what was happening. The pressure of his grip almost sent her to her knees.

"Don't you ever talk to me like that again." His lip was curled up in a snarl, and his eyes were beady and squinted. "You and that worthless, piss-ant son of yours are gonna pay. You have no idea who you are dealing with, little missy." While he had her in his grip, he reared back his fist and planted it directly into Hannah Frye's right eye. He hit her with brute force, and Hannah was pretty sure her eye socket cracked.

Butch released his grip on her arm and purposefully let her drop to the floor in a heap. Without another word, he walked out Hannah's front door, slamming it behind him so hard it jarred the pictures hanging on the wall.

Hannah Frye was sprawled flat on her back in the front foyer. The room was spinning, and the pain was sharp. It didn't take her long to realize a stream of blood was flowing from her cheek. She reached for the arm of the chair next to the door and pulled herself slowly up on her wobbly legs. Her mouth began to water as if she was going to vomit, however, Hannah was already going into all out "Hannah" mode. She knew she had to think straight and make sound decisions on what she needed to do from there.

Attempting a logical conversation with herself while her head was throbbing was a challenge, however, Hannah decided the best thing for her to do was to go to the emergency room. Hopefully, they could do some magic and fix her up before Mookie saw her looking like she had been hit by a truck. Even though her head was pounding, reality was not lost on her. Mookie Frye was a lot like his father but had a temper like his mom.

Convinced she was able to drive, Hannah got her purse and moved unsteadily toward her truck. She controlled the steering wheel in one hand and held a towel up to her bleeding face with the other.

The hospital was five miles away from their farm. She decided to take the back way, in case she weaved a bit. The last thing she needed was to be pulled over by the police.

Thankfully, she made it to the hospital without a hitch, and found a good parking place near the emergency room entrance.

As she reached for her purse, Hannah heard a voice inside her head. The voice reminded her that Mookie was going to be pitching in the state championship baseball game tomorrow. There was a certainty that scouts would be coming from all over to watch him pitch. If she went into the emergency room tonight and got stitches and had bandages all over her face, there would be no way that Mookie would be in the right frame of mind to pitch like he needed to pitch to win the championship. She could be ruining his chances for a future in baseball. Stick always said that Mookie should be able to have his chance. Come hell or high water, Mookie shouldn't be robbed of his future.

Hannah made the decision to go back home and do her best to cover her injuries. She didn't want to think past that, she knew she had to take it one step at a time, but the bottom-line was, Mookie wasn't going to find out what happened to her, at least not until after the ball game.

The ride back to the farm had Hannah deep in thought. Her mind was whirling, thinking about Butch and what he had done to her, all the while trying to concoct a plan in case she wasn't successful in hiding the injuries to her face.

Still in a daze, Hannah walked up her porch steps, looked up and saw that her front door was standing wide open. Had she left in such a fog that she forgot to close the door?

CHAPTER 67

Soggy Cereal and the News

It was almost eleven o'clock when Mookie got home that night. He had left the Allen's around nine-thirty, but after hanging out with his friends, and flashing Frosty sweet smiles every time she walked past the door to the den, Mookie just didn't feel like going straight home. He was excited about the possibility of being "three-peat" state champions tomorrow, he had such a joy in his heart thinking about a future with Frosty, and, with the exception of his mom's looming wedding to Butch Baxter, life in general just seemed to be rocking along in his favor. Rolling the windows down and cranking up the volume on his truck radio as he sang along to his favorite country songs, Mookie had the world by the tail, at least for an hour or so.

It was so muddy everywhere from the steady rain during the week, Mookie had to keep his truck from sliding sideways as he drove down the dirt and gravel driveway toward the house. It was quiet inside and

Hannah had left the hallway light on for Mookie before she went to bed. Mookie tiptoed to his room to call it a night, falling fast asleep as soon as his head hit the pillow.

The next thing he heard was his radio alarm with Denny Matthews giving the recap of the Kansas City Royals baseball game from the night before.

He thought he heard his mother in the hallway and it sounded like she was crying.

"Hey, mom, you ok?" He hollered from his bedroom.

"Yes, honey, I am," She answered back. "When you get dressed, your cereal is ready. It's your big day!" Hannah had muffled her crying, determined to sound as cheerful as always. Mookie decided maybe he had heard one of the barnyard cats outside his window, so he finished listening to Denny Matthews while he put on his clothes. Just as he started to turn off the radio, the local news came on with a report of a fire in Blackjack Hollow. The reporter relayed to the listeners that the local Liquor Store had burned to the ground. He stated that the fire department had gotten a call around ten-thirty the night before, alerting them that the building was fully engulfed in flames. There were no injuries, however, the building was a total loss. At the conclusion of the report, Mookie smiled and slowly turned off his radio. The liquor store was a pile of ashes and Mookie couldn't be happier.

Sitting at the kitchen table, he knew he couldn't put it off any longer. Mookie poured his bowl of soggy Cap'n Crunch cereal into the garbage disposal, turned it on, and watched as the last of the yellow bits got whirled, devoured, and swished away into the drain.

"Mom, I've got to go to school in ten minutes. Please come out of your room. I saw your face." Mookie was matter of fact as he stood at the door to his mother's room.

"Mookie, I feel so stupid. I did the dumbest thing." Hannah opened her door and faced her son, full on, baring her swollen and bruised face.

"Mom! Oh my God! What happened to you?" Mookie looked at his mom with horror.

"I did the stupidest thing. I was embarrassed to tell you. I promise I will go to the doctor tomorrow, but it feels better, and I didn't want to miss a second of your game."

"So, tell me, Mom. You look awful." Mookie put his hand on his mother's hair, smoothing it as he talked.

"When I got home from the hardware store, I grabbed the new door latch and went out to the chicken coop to take the old one off and put the new one on. When I pulled on the door to the coop to open it, the rest of the rusty latch broke away and the door came flying off and hit me in the face. Now, go on to school. You need to be there by eight-thirty to catch the bus to Tulsa and you don't want to be late. The coaches might bench ya!" She giggled, patted Mookie on the back and gently pushed him away from her room.

"Okay, mom. I guess I'm glad you didn't get hurt worse, but please let me do the manly stuff around here. Oh, and are you gonna wear some really big sunglasses today?" He winked and smiled at his mom as he turned to go to school.

Hannah followed her son outside, stood on the porch and shouted out to Mookie as he drove away, "I'll see you in Tulsa, Mookie. Go Blackjack Hollow! Take State!"

Mookie's Ford Ranger eventually became a speck in the distance, and when she was convinced he was far enough down the road that he couldn't see her, Hannah slid down into Stick's red wooden rocking chair and cried. She cried until she couldn't cry any more, then she went into the house to get ready to drive to Tulsa for the baseball game.

As she stepped into the shower, Hannah told herself to get a grip. She knew full well that Butch Baxter's butt would be planted on a prominent seat in the bleachers today. She also knew she couldn't let him get the upper hand.

After drying off from her shower, Hannah looked fixedly at the swollen face staring back at her in the mirror. The events of the night before seemed like a dream or a nightmare, however, her bruises begged to differ. Butch Baxter was evil. He was an evil man. As that reality washed over her, an acute feeling of fear brought chills to her body. He was dangerous for sure, but she was smarter. Hannah was convinced that she had more smarts in her little finger than Butch Baxter had in his entire body. She resolved to not let him win and vowed that she would not let fear overtake her wits. "Dear God, I'm asking you to please show me what I need to do. And, Stick, honey, if you can help me in any way, I need you now more than ever." As she spoke to her reflection in the mirror, Hannah was suddenly overcome by an eerie feeling. It was as if someone was trying to tell her something. The voice from within kept repeating, "Save Mookie." Any remaining fear was instantly replaced with fury. With both hands on the counter, Hannah leaned in toward the mirror and said, "Hannah Frye, you need to outsmart Butch Baxter. No one is going to hurt your son."

CHAPTER 68:

Mookie on the Mound

The Blackjack Hollow Bulldogs took the field first, for warm-ups. Coach Pierce had delivered a rousing motivational speech, like no other, bestowing upon them the confidence to give it their all and handily send their opponent home, empty handed.

Much to Mookie's surprise, the fielding practice was going smoothly as Butch Ed Baxter stood calmly and collectively at his third base position, scooping up line drives, and snagging pop flies, courteously tossing them back to Mookie, without incident.

Mookie told himself to just stay focused. Even though Butch Ed seemed to be exhibiting a good effort of teamwork at the moment, Mookie didn't trust him any farther than he could throw him. The other shoe could drop anytime, and Mookie didn't want to be blindsided. "Just stay focused on winning this game," Mookie told himself, over and over.

It hadn't rained as much in Tulsa as it had around Blackjack Hollow, therefore the field was in perfect shape. The sun was high in the sky, giving the grass in the ball field a vivid, emerald glow. The dirt around the mound was raked to a fine powder, allowing Mookie's cleats to press lightly into the surface as he made his way to take his pitching stance. The rubber on the mound was like an old friend. Mookie Frye was meant to be a pitcher. Just like his dad.

The diamond-shaped pattern of a baseball infield elevates the pitcher on the raised mound. Not to single him out as more important than the rest of the team, but to signify that the play begins with the release of the cork-filled, leather-bound baseball. A championship caliber ball team must think ahead of each pitch, anticipating their own reactions to accurately execute the best plan to send the opposing team's batter, and any players standing on the bases, back to the dugout. The Blackjack Hollow Bulldogs took the field first and were preparing to make that happen.

All players were in their positions as Mookie Frye made his way to the mound. Blowing bubbles with the generous amount of Big League Chew bubble gum he had socked in his mouth kept Mookie's mind off anything happening outside the fence surrounding the baseball field. He was mentally prepared and zeroed in on his mission to have precise accuracy with each ball that left his hand.

Thankfully, there was a light breeze blowing that afternoon, keeping the stifling humidity at bay.

Stomping on the rubber with his head down, making sure his feet were planted exactly the way he wanted them to be, Mookie appeared to be lost in a pitch-perfecting ritual. Contrary to the spectators' perception, Mookie's ceremonial custom, without fail, was a one-sided, silent conversation with his father, Stick Frye, "This game is for you, Dad. You taught me everything you knew. You will always be my hero and my

246

role-model for being a great pitcher and an even greater man. I hope I'm making you proud."

He raised his head slowly and scanned the stands. Mookie's heart skipped a beat as he located Frosty. Their eyes met as she flashed him a sweet smile, fluttering her three fingers at him in a cutesy wave. He returned her gestures with a smile and a wink. Frosty was sitting by his mom, Hannah. Hannah blew him a kiss and a confident "thumbs up." Trying not to lose his concentration, Mookie couldn't help but notice Butch Baxter perched in a seat higher up in the stands. He thought to himself, "That's odd that he's not sitting with my mom, but that's their problem. Maybe mom is getting her brain back."

The umpire behind the batter's box was bent over, sweeping any lingering dirt away from home plate. Mookie held his glove up to his chin with his left hand, his right hand was placed just inside the pocket, hiding his finger placement on the ball, as he didn't want to give away his choice for his first pitch.

"Batter up!" The umpire called out as he moved back into position behind Stoney Allen. Stoney and Mookie had already sent each other their secret signals and the state championship game was ready to commence.

Just as Mookie stepped backward to hurl the ball, Coach Pierce came out of the dugout, putting his left hand up to the umpire, telling him to hold up the game. As the coach walked with determination toward the mound, he was followed by two uniformed, county deputies. The umpire motioned to the batter to step away from the batter's box and held both hands in the air as he shouted, "Time!"

Coach Pierce approached Mookie with a look of confusion as he escorted the two officers to the mound.

"Milton Frye?" One of the deputies said as he stepped toward Mookie.

"Yes, sir. I am Milton Frye." Mookie dropped his glove to his side.

The second deputy pulled a set of handcuffs from his back pocket. He dutifully walked behind Mookie, bringing the young man's arms together behind his back, securing the handcuffs around Mookie's wrists. The officer looked directly at Mookie as he began to speak, "Milton Frye, I am Tulsa County deputy, Oren Sparks. This here is Roger's County Deputy, Ken Olsen. I am informing you that you are being placed under arrest as you have been charged with first degree arson. The alleged crime occurred in Rogers County, therefore, you will be handed over to Deputy Olsen to be transported to the Rogers County jail."

Deputy Olsen spoke next. "Milton Fry, you have the right to remain silent. Anything you say can and will be used against you in a court of law. You have the right to talk to an attorney and have him present with you as you are being questioned. If you cannot afford an attorney, one will be appointed for you by the court."

Mookie Frye showed no emotions. As the deputies ushered him off the field, he looked toward the stands. His mother and Frosty were hurriedly making their way down the steps, Butch Baxter was standing in his spot covering a dropped-jaw smirk with his hand, and, lastly, Mookie's heart sank as his eyes turned to the left side of the bleachers. Representatives from the Kansas City Royals, John Wathan and George Brett, were walking out of the stadium, toward the parking lot.

CHAPTER 69:

The Mugshot

The deputy photographer stood Mookie in front of a long poster. Height labels were printed along the right side of the paper, designating by the position of the top of Mookie's head that he was exactly six feet tall.

"Milton, I need you to turn to the left now. Got it. Now to the right." Mookie's mugshots were finished just as Deputy Olsen came into the room.

"Your attorney is here, Milton. He's waiting in that room on the left, so, I'm gonna take the cuffs off you while you're in there. If you know what's good for you, I expect no funny business."

"Thank you, sir." Mookie turned his back to the deputy and raised his arms the best he could. The key was inserted, and his wrists were released from the constraints of the metal rings that were pinching the skin around his wrists.

He rubbed his wrists to relieve the pain as Deputy Olsen took him by the elbow and led him into the small, cubicle-like room.

A middle-aged gentleman in a gray suit stood up from behind the table in the room and stuck his hand out toward Mookie.

"Milton, or I suppose you would like to be called Mookie. Mookie, come on in and sit right here in this chair." He pointed to the chair across the table from his seat. "My name is Don Wiseman. I was raised in Tishomingo and am a long-time friend of your dad's. Your mother, Hannah, has retained me to represent you in this case."

Mookie was consoled to learn that his new attorney had family ties.

"Okay, Mr. Wiseman, if you're a friend of my dad's, I consider that to be in my favor."

Mr. Wiseman jumped in with both feet.

"Before we get started, I need to make sure you understand the severity of the crime they're charging you with, son. First degree arson is a felony. Felonies can carry a sentence of at least a year in jail, maybe more. Mookie, do you understand the hot water you are in, being charged with a first degree, felony?"

"Honestly Mr. Wiseman, I don't have a clue about anything they're sayin'. I know what they mean by arson, but what the heck is it that they are sayin' I set fire to? I don't have a clue what they're talkin' about." A tear slid down Mookie's cheek.

"All right then, let's get this straight before we go any farther. If I am going to help you, son, you must trust me enough to tell me the God's truth. All of it. Don't leave a single detail out and I promise you that I will go to the wall to help you. I owe it to your dad. That man never ever walked away from helping me or anyone. Quite frankly, I owe my life to Stick Frye." Don Wiseman, leaned toward Mookie with both fists clenched on the table. "They are saying you burned down the Liquor Store in Blackjack Hollow. Did you or did you not set fire to that store and burn it to the ground? I will leave this room and never come back if you don't tell me the truth."

"What? They think I'm the one that set fire to the Liquor Store? Seriously? Why do they think I did it? This is just crazy!" Mookie was incredulous. "Mr. Wiseman, I swear to you on the grave of my dead father, I did not burn down the Liquor Store."

"I believe you, Mookie. I do believe you." Mr. Wiseman sat back in the chair and folded his arms across his chest. "We will get a game plan. Sit tight here in this jail and keep your nose clean. We go before the judge at eight o'clock tomorrow morning. If, unfortunately, he concurs with the prosecution that you are to be bound over for trial, I will request that you be released in your mother's custody, with a minimum bail. You don't have a record, so that should be easy enough to accomplish. I see we have Judge Gambill. He's fair and a straight shooter. So, for now, I'm going to step out here and request a meeting with the district attorney and get a feel for why they are coming after you. They wouldn't have charged you without some pretty convincing evidence. I'll look at what they have and see if we can get to work knocking a big hole in their case. I'll be back here at seven in the morning. We will sit down together again before we go in to Judge Gambill's courtroom. Hopefully, I will have some good news by morning." Mr. Wiseman shook Mookie's hand and walked toward the door. Before he continued on his way out, he turned back toward Mookie, hesitated, then spoke.

"I have to admit to you, Mookie, I almost feel spooked. You are the spitting image of your dad. Like his twin and while we were sitting there, for a moment, it was like he was in there with us. I could almost feel his presence." Mr. Wiseman stood for a second longer, looked back around the room, and left.

CHAPTER 70:

Beyond a Resonable Doubt

Mookie didn't get to talk to his mom until six thirty, the morning of the hearing. They exchanged tight hugs, with Hannah assuring Mookie that Dan Wiseman was the best attorney money could buy, and he was taking Mookie's case pro bono. Mr. Wiseman told Hannah that he wouldn't even think of taking a penny of her money to defend the son of Stick Frye. Stick Frye had actually saved Dan Wiseman's life when they were teenagers. Mr. Wiseman had told Hannah that one hot, summer day, they were jumping off a train trestle into a river, when Dan's foot got caught in the tracks. A train was fast approaching, and Stick Frye came out of nowhere, freeing Dan's foot, grabbing Dan and jumping tandem with him into the water. Just in the nick of time.

Mookie was proud to hear that story about his dad. However, before he could say another word, Mr. Wiseman came around the corner of the courthouse hallway.

His brow was furrowed, and his pace was quick.

"Hannah, Mookie, step inside this room with me. I need to go over a few things with you both."

It was serious. Brutally serious. The district attorney's office informed Mr. Wiseman that they had very damaging evidence which, as far as they were concerned, pointed an air-tight, slam-dunk finger at Mookie Frye.

To begin with, the circumstantial evidence was damning. Mookie Frye was notorious in Blackjack Hollow for being a staunch, and outspoken, teetotaler. The DA's office went down the list of reasons why Mookie would want to see the Liquor Store destroyed. There was gossip around town that his father's accident was caused by alcohol. Furthermore, Mookie had recently lost a close friend in a drunk driving accident, thereby personally founding a local chapter of Students Against Drunk Driving in his friend's name. All very detrimental to Mookie's defense.

Mr. Wiseman explained to Mookie and Hannah that circumstantial evidence was just what it said it was and did not normally bring a conviction if it stood alone. Unfortunately for Mookie, the prosecution had physical evidence, that they arrogantly shoved across the desk to Mr. Wiseman, touting that the key was practically in the lock to send Mookie to jail.

"Mookie, do you own a pair of cowboy boots with the letters "BF" embossed on the front?"

"Yes, sir, I do. They belonged to my late grandfather, Boots Frye. I wear them to every rodeo. Why?" Mookie was having a hard time understanding what his granddad's boots had to do with anything.

"Mookie, they have your boots. They were found stuck in the mud at the scene of the crime. They are convinced that in the process of committing the crime, you got spooked and tried to run away. Thinking someone was on your tail, they believe you sank down into the mud, got stuck, so you yanked your feet out and ran. If that's not bad enough, Mookie, they also have an opened bag of some kind of shredded bubble gum," Mr. Wiseman glanced down at his notes. "I guess it's called Big League Chew? Apparently, the bag has your name on it. Let's see, it's here in my notes. Written on the bag is, 'To Mookie Frye, Best wishes for a successful baseball career. And it's signed by, Rob Nelson, Portland Mavericks, Pitcher. The prosecution is prepared to convince the judge that the bubble gum package fell out of your pocket when you hurried away from the scene of the crime." Mr. Wiseman exhaled deeply, "I have to tell you, both, we've got our work set out for us. This does not look good at all. We will have to get our heads together soon. My biggest worry today is if Judge Gambill will even let you out on bail. Let's head into the court room." Mr. Wiseman bent over the table to gather his notes. As he was shuffling the papers, he glanced up at Mookie, "Mookie, we better be thinking about your alibi. The arson investigators have estimated that the fire started around ten o'clock Thursday night. Where were you at that time?"

Mookie put his head down and raised it slowly, realizing the futility of his answer.

"I was driving around in my truck. By myself."

Mr. Wiseman closed his eyes, took a deep breath, then shook his head.

"Let's go face Judge Gambill."

CHAPTER 71

Boots Frye's Legacy and the Beholden Deputy

Hannah Frye was devastated. Judge Gambill denied bail for Mookie, tersely instructing him that he would be sitting in the county jail until his trial date, which was placed on the court docket ninety days away. Not only was she heartbroken at the thought of her eighteen-year-old son being locked behind bars with varying degrees of lewd and crazy adult criminals, Hannah was saddened by the fact that his future in baseball was being circumvented, he would not be able to escort Frosty to the prom, and, almost too sad to think about, was the fact that Mookie wouldn't be able to attend his high school graduation. It was the embodiment of unfairness.

No matter how hard he tried, Mookie couldn't go to sleep. It wasn't because loud snoring was erupting from nearly every cell, or because the jailers on duty were laughing and talking in an office only ten feet from him, and it wasn't even because he was upset at his predicament. The reason he couldn't sleep was simply that his mind was racing a hundred miles an hour. He was innocent, and someone had gone to a lot of trouble to frame him for something he didn't do. Who and why? Who held a grudge against him so forceful that they would want to ruin his life and see him sent to jail? Who would that be? He couldn't think of anyone that hated him that badly. Butch Ed was mean to him and pretty ticked over the deal with Frosty, but Mookie just chalked that up to immaturity and jealousy on Butch Ed's part. "Butch Ed would never go that far. He's not very smart and is way too much of a weenie."

Every detail of the conversation with Mr. Wiseman kept turning over and over in his mind. The evidence. The crafty criminal had to have given a lot of thought and planning in setting up the crime scene to present such an airtight case against him. He had to give them that one right off the top.

The incriminating evidence. No matter how hard he tried to focus on the evidence, as he knew it was crucial to be smarter than the crook, there was one statement that kept coming back to his brain and he couldn't shake it no matter how hard he tried.

"There was gossip around town that his father's accident was caused by alcohol."

Why did that haunt him? Why?

He suddenly remembered the dream. His dad and granddad came to him and warned him about the burning Liquor Store! "Dad and Granddad, what were you trying to show me? The burning Liquor Store and the beer cans. Dad and Granddad, are you there? Please help me."

"Milton, are you awake?" Mookie was lying on his back in the lower bunk when he turned his head and saw a shadowy figure looming outside the jail cell. He sat straight up, straining his eyes to see who it was.

"Yes, sir, I am." Mookie got up from the bed and walked toward the man. He immediately recognized him as the night shift jail deputy.

"Milton, my name is Pee Wee. Pee Wee Ferguson. I just had to come out here and talk to you. I've been in there in the office sortin' through case evidence boxes that need to be transferred to storage, and when I lifted one of the boxes up on the table, well, I had quite a surprise. I have to tell you, my eyes bugged right outta my head when I came across a pair of boots out there in a box that has your name on it. I would recognize those boots anywhere. I've been retired from the rodeo circuit, I guess goin' on about twenty years now, and I've got to ask you, how in the heck do you know Boots Frye?" Pee Wee leaned forward and his eyes narrowed as he tried to wrap his mind around seeing Boots Frye's cowboy boots in a cardboard box in the county jail in Claremore, Oklahoma. Who was this kid, anyway?

"Well, sir, Boots Frye, was my granddad. He's my dad's father."

"What the heck? Are you kiddin' me? You are Stick's son?" Pee Wee moved in closer and held his flashlight up to Mookie's face. "Well, I'll be gall darned! You are the spittin' image of ol' Stick-tight Frye. Son, I want you to know that your granddaddy is the reason I am still standing here, alive and well, on this earth today. Boots saved my life nigh on forty years ago. We used to ride the rodeo circuit together and I can rightly say, Boots Frye was one of the finest men God ever put on this earth. We rode the bulls and did team ropin' together. He was the header, and I was the heeler. One time we were in a rodeo over at Chickasaw. We had already won our team ropin' event and were pretty pleased with our individual standins' on the leaderboard goin' in to the finals in the bull ridin'. Ol'

Boots hung for a solid eight, and I was up next. I remember this like it was yesterday, son, when I came outta the chute, the dang ol' bull did a reverse and I slid right off his side. Bad thang was, my spur got caught in the bull's flank strap and that idiot was whippin' me around like a rag doll. I thought fer sure I was a goner, and then outta nowhere comes Boots Frye. He rode a horse out there and somehow, only the good Lord knows, he was able to jump from the horse to the back of that ol' bull and loosen my spur. Yep, your granddaddy saved this ol' sorry son of a buck's life."

"Wow! That's just crazy! I'm so glad to meet you, Mr. Ferguson. And please just call me Mookie. I'd be hard pressed to disagree with you about my granddad, and my dad for that matter. They will always be my heroes." Mookie was in amazement thinking about what the chances were that one of the jailers knew his dad, and granddad. And he recognized the boots!

"All right then, Mookie it is. And you just call me Pee Wee. No Mr. Ferguson allowed. I've got to get back to work, but before I go, I want to tell you, I don't know the particulars of why a kid from such a good family is sittin' here in my jail, but somethin' tells me you ain't supposed to be here. Boots Frye saved my life and I owe a debt of gratitude to him. He's gone now so there's nothin' I can do directly for him, but Mookie, whatever it is, if you need anything, rest assured that I will do my best to see to it that you are taken good care of while you are here with me. Let me know if you need anything." With that, Pee Wee Ferguson walked away into the dark of the night.

The miracle of what had just transpired was not lost on Mookie. He had both hands wrapped around the bars on his cell, looked up to the ceiling and said, "Thanks, Dad and Granddad. I knew it. You never leave me."

CHAPTER 72

Cashin' in with Stoney

Hannah Frye was on her way to the jail to visit Mookie. She had just gotten released from the hospital after having to stay there two days for an infection that had set in around her injured eye. Luckily, she didn't require stitches and when they got the infection under control, the swelling subsided, and the bruising was starting to fade. Finally, Hannah was very pleased to see her normal face when she looked in the mirror.

She was so anxious to be able to see her son, she was driving ten miles over the speed limit. There were no cops in her rearview mirror, and for that she was certainly relieved.

"Mrs. Frye!" Hannah was walking toward the jail when she looked over her shoulder and saw Frosty and her parents. Frosty ran over toward Hannah and they gave each other big hugs. "We just left, Mookie, Mrs. Frye. He seems to be holding up really well." Frosty's eyes began to fill with tears. "It's so hard for me to see him locked up in there. I still can't believe this is happening to him." Hannah reached into her purse and pulled out a tissue for Frosty.

"We're going to get him out of there, Frosty. Keep praying. We won't stop until he walks out of that door over there."

They said their goodbyes and Frosty assured Hannah that she and her parents would be back to see Mookie again the next day.

Seventeen steps. Hannah couldn't believe that she had become so familiar with the court house that she knew there were seventeen steps up to the front door. She never thought she would ever know so much about the inside of the court house. Never in a million years did she ever think she would have to go down to the basement of the old building to visit her son in jail. Never in a million years.

"Mom! You look so much better. Thank God." Mookie was so glad to see his mother, he grabbed her up in a big bear hug. "You can put away those big sunglasses now." He and Hannah laughed.

Hannah was happy to see that Mookie was in such a good mood. He reminded her so much of Stick. No matter how bad things were, nobody could steal their joy.

"Mom, can you sit down? I want to talk to you about somethin'. I've been doin' a lot of thinkin'. Yeah, of course I've been doin' a lot of thinkin'." He laughed at that. "So, Mom, I want to tell you I'm sorry about the way I acted about you and your relationship with Butch. I've been such a brat about it all. I feel so bad now that I look back on everything. I promise I will do better from here on out."

Hannah reached over and grabbed Mookie's hand.

"Mook, I think there's only one good reason God has you sitting here in this jail."

Mookie furrowed his brow. Where was his mom going with this?

262

"Son, I think you are here because what I am getting ready to tell you would send you on a rampage. God wanted you locked up, so you wouldn't do anything stupid. Now don't worry, we're going to get you out of here in no time." Hannah continued, "Mookie. You were right all along about Butch Baxter. He is pure evil." Hannah reached for his other hand and held them both with a tight grip. She looked directly into her son's eyes and said, "Butch Baxter hit me in the eye. And he is out to get us. He wants to destroy us both."

Mookie tried to pull his hands away, so he could get up from the table and hit somebody, but Hannah held on tight. "Mookie, Mook, hang on. We've got to be smart. Think about it. Butch wants us to do something stupid. We can't let him win."

Mookie knew she was right. They had to be smarter than Butch.

Then it hit him. Right between the eyes.

"Mom, I need you to go out there right now and find Deputy Ferguson. Deputy Pee Wee Ferguson. He just came on duty. He's a good guy, I will tell you more about him later, but right now we've got to hurry. When you find the deputy, ask him if we can get Stoney in here. We need to get Stoney in here right away."

Hannah flew out the door and headed down the hall. Deputy Ferguson came through with flying colors and Stoney Allen was in the jail office in no time.

Mookie was so overjoyed to see his best friend, and the feeling was mutual. They had been able to talk on the phone a few times, but it was such a relief to have Stoney standing in the same room with him.

"Mom, something has been bugging me and now I get why. Do you remember something Mr. Wiseman said during our meeting? He told us the prosecution said there was gossip around town that Dad's accident was alcohol related."

Hannah nodded slowly as she tried to see where Mookie was going with this.

"Mom, the coroner was from out of town. Remember, when we looked at Dad's death certificate there was nothing on there about alcohol being a factor in the accident? In our grief, we were just glad it wasn't on there and we just wanted to move on. What if the coroner didn't see anything alcohol related when he came and looked at Dad's body? Butch Baxter is the only one that ever said anything about alcohol, and he waited until the sheriff was out of the room before he brought it up. If there was gossip spread around town about Dad's accident being alcohol related, there's only one person that could have started it."

Hannah put her hand to her mouth, as Mookie continued.

"Stoney, this is where you come in. Can you think of anything that we can do? We are good private eyes. We've had a lot of experience on accidents scenes..."

Hannah's eyes got big, "Mookie, what in the world are you talking about? What do you mean you and Stoney have experience on accident scenes? I thought you just did chicken coops."

"Mom, I will explain more later. Now's not the time. So, Stoney, can you think of anything?"

Stoney Allen thought a moment, then his eyes almost popped out of his head.

"Oh my gosh, Mook! I get it now. This is all so crazy! So, a couple of days after your dad died, I had the weirdest dream. In the dream you and I were doing an accident scene. I was down on my hands and knees pouring the plaster in the tracks. You were wandering around looking at things and picking stuff up and putting them in a box. Suddenly, I looked up and you were gone, and it was your dad picking stuff up. He said, "Stoney, we have to do this to help Mookie." When I woke up, I was kinda scared at first, then it was weird, because I just decided to go over to your field and do the investigation by myself. Everything was just like the deputies left it and it just seemed right at the time. I was thinking that if doing the scene of your dad's accident helped you in any way, I would do it. I found some things there and put them in a box. It's in our garage. I didn't want to tell you because I didn't want to upset you."

"Oh my gosh, Stoney. That's terrific! You're terrific! Okay, Mom, please go clear it with Deputy Ferguson, and see if it's okay if Stoney leaves here and brings back the box from dad's accident."

Hannah jumped up to go find the deputy, when Stoney spoke again, "Mookie, as long as I'm getting it all out here, well, I also did an investigation of the scene of the fire at the liquor store. I got some plaster footprints."

Mookie leapt from his chair and encircled his buddy, Stoney, in a huge hug. They gave each other a big high five, and Hannah and Stoney ran out the door.

CHAPTER 73

Beer Can, Baseball Bat, Rope and Booze

Charley Bowman sometimes found "gifts" when he went to check on the wash pan on his Saturday morning strolls, and there was no doubt in his mind that Bigfoot was the one leaving them for him. The first time was the beer can. Charley put it on a shelf in his shed. He didn't know why he was keeping it, but there on the shelf it sat. A few days after the beer can showed up, Charley went to the old stump and lying crosswise on the top of the aluminum wash pan was a wooden baseball bat. It was cracked, and embedded in the crack were several long, red hairs and a few speckles, which Charley thought could possibly be blood. When the baseball bat showed up, Charley considered taking it into town to the police station. That thought left quickly as he remembered how the townspeople had ridiculed him over the Bigfoot incident. He just wanted to mind his own business and stay as far away from that town as possible. Charley placed the baseball bat on the same shelf as the beer can and walked away.

Bigfoot continued to enjoy his Friday night feasts, but it was almost a year until another item was left by the wash pan on the stump. One Saturday morning, as usual, Charley Bowman, strolled out by the stump to look in the wash pan. To his surprise there was a piece of rope rolled up inside the pan. The rope found a home on the shelf with the beer can and the baseball bat. Charley concluded that Bigfoot was a junk collector and thinking that the hairy animal was bringing his benefactor a token of his appreciation for the food was somewhat humorous to Charley Bowman.

It wasn't until the latest items showed up, that Charley Bowman began to get alarmed. Instead of finding an empty aluminum pan, there were four charred bottles of vodka standing upright in the middle.

He had just read the Saturday morning edition of the Blackjack Hollow Bugle. His friend, Mookie Frye, had been arrested the day before, and was charged with first degree arson. They were accusing him of burning down the Liquor Store.

CHAPTER 74:

Edwinna Is Not a Kook

"Edwinna, this is Annie Bowman. Yes, I am doing quite well, dear. And you? That's great. Well, Annie, the reason for my call is, I was wondering if you might have some time today to stop by our house. Charley has just shared some disturbing information with me and we believe you might find it interesting. Oh, my, yes, two o'clock will be wonderful. I'll have some hot tea and snickerdoodles ready for an afternoon snack."

Charley Bowman told Annie everything. Even though she was in shock that her husband had actually seen the creature with his own eyes, she was relieved that Charley hadn't been the one eating all of the coconut cream pie. "With his sugar diabetes and all."

Edwinna Blackworth, took notes as Charley ticked off every detail of the happenings around the old stump over the years.

"Charley, you know I have never doubted you a bit. This is the most exciting thing I believe I have ever heard! Bigfoot is real, and he has a personality! First and foremost, I agree with Annie. You must turn the items in to the authorities. Especially if there is any way it could help that sweet child, Mookie Frye. We all know that is a set up. Something is definitely rotten in Denmark! Charley, I understand your reluctance, as you have every right to hold a grudge against those people. You know that I, of all people, understand what it's like to be ridiculed. I could absolutely wring that Buddy Tempey's neck. Calling me a kook! I never!"

Charley, Annie, and Edwinna, agreed that the best way to go was to call Hannah and see what she wanted them to do.

CHAPTER 75:

The Tables are Turned

Deputy Ferguson's curiosity had gotten the better of him, so he wanted to be in the room when Stoney Allen brought in the two boxes of investigation items. Hannah and Mookie were anxious to see what Stoney found at the farm when he investigated Stick's accident scene, but they were also overtaken with sadness as the memories of his death were brought to light.

Stoney opened the flaps to the box and started setting things on the table. There were a couple of wrenches, some cotter pins, and baling wire that had probably fell out of the tractor's tool box when it turned over. He hesitated a moment before he took out the rest. One by one Stoney set out empty beer cans.

Hannah gasped. Mookie thought she was having a nervous breakdown and almost sent Stoney for a medic.

"Mom! Mom, are you okay? I know this is so upsetting to you. I'm so sorry. Maybe you shouldn't have seen this. He didn't mean to drink. I know he's sorry."

"Mookie! Oh my God! I think your dad might have been murdered! I'm thinking Butch Baxter might have killed your dad!" Hannah held her hands up to her mouth. She was horror-struck.

"What? What are you talking about? What makes you think that?" Mookie and Stoney rushed toward Hannah.

"Mookie, your dad was deathly allergic to beer. He only drank beer once in his life and it sent him to the hospital. No one knew about that around here but your dad and me. His death was set up to look like he got drunk and turned over the tractor. If it had truly been an accident there wouldn't have been any reason to spread beer cans everywhere. The murderer didn't know he was allergic to beer. We've got to nail that bastard, Butch Baxter to the wall."

CHAPTER 76

The Revelation

"Stoney, let's look at the other box." Mookie's head was spinning. They had to find more proof.

The box from the Liquor Store fire smelled like smoke.

"There wasn't much left around the store since everything burned to the ground, but, as I was walking around, I saw a couple of holes in the mud. I guess that's where they found the cowboy boots and pulled them out of the mud. I saw a couple of footprints on the outside of the holes. Maybe that was where whoever was wearing the boots took their feet out to leave the boots behind. The footprints then came together and left a trail of prints. I got several good ones, Mookie. Take a look." Stoney lifted the white plaster from the cardboard box and set them out on the table.

Mookie, Hannah and Deputy Ferguson moved closer to the table to take a better look.

Mookie Frye banged his fists on the table. "This is it! I can't believe it. We've got 'em! Oh my gosh, there it is." Mookie pointed toward the plaster casts.

"Each footprint is missing the big toe. We've just nailed Butch Ed Baxter!"

Deputy Ferguson moved closer to the table, "I'm not real sure I understand much of what is goin' on here, but I guarantee I can get Sheriff Stonecipher to take a look at this. I was talkin' to him the other night and he told me he just found out his cousin, Roy Dell Barnes, was in the same rodeo as your dad when your dad got hurt. Roy Dell lives just a couple of miles from here."

Sheriff Stonecipher came in the next morning and sat with Mookie, Stoney, and Hannah. They explained everything they had discovered, and Hannah also brought in a box from Charley Bowman, with the items he gave her. However, she conveniently left out the part of Charley's story about Bigfoot. She didn't want anything to stand in the way of getting justice for her son and bringing up Bigfoot may not bode well for Mookie.

Fortunately for Mookie, Sheriff Stonecipher thought a lot of what he had been shown was worthy of more investigation and gave orders to one of his deputies to bring Butch Ed Baxter in for questioning. The plaster casts were the most solid piece of evidence. Since Butch Ed was only eighteen they would lean on him hard and see if they could get him to talk.

CHAPTER 77:

He Sang Like a Bird

As soon as they showed Butch Ed Baxter the plaster footprints, he folded like an accordion.

After Sheriff Stonecipher let Hannah and Mookie listen to the recording of Butch Ed's confession, they were consumed with a mixture of emotions. They felt sorry for Butch Ed, but they felt heartbroken for themselves more.

"Butch Ed, you have stated that you do not want an attorney present. You are of legal age and you have the right to refuse counsel. Therefore, you have agreed to give your confession and you have agreed to allow us to tape record your confession. I need you to state your name, give us your age and address and just start telling the tape recorder what you just told us." The deputy signaled to Butch Ed that the recorder was on and ready for him to speak into the microphone.

"My name is Butch Edward Baxter. I'm eighteen. No wait, I just had my birthday. I'm nineteen years old. I live in Blackjack Hollow,

Oklahoma. Rt 7 Box 242. Now do I just start talking? Okay. When I was nine years old, we had just moved to Blackjack Hollow. My mom was sick. She was mentally ill. I think they called it manic depression and agoraphobia. My dad made fun of her all the time. She never cried though. I never understood that part. When we moved to Blackjack Hollow, my dad would make me go with him all the time to look through his binoculars at Hannah Frye. We would park in the woods by our house and we could see the Frye's farm really good from there and not be seen by them. He told me every day that she was the kind of woman that we needed instead of a crazy woman like my mom. He was always saying, "Look at Hannah. She's always dressed nice, her hair is fixed cute, and she's always helping do things on the farm. Now, that, Butch Ed, is the perfect woman." We did that every day until the day he made me kill my mom. He had been yelling at her all day. I tried to stay outside as much as I could. He kept drinking beer all day long and got so drunk he could hardly walk. He came outside around ten o'clock and told me to drive the truck to the bluffs and he would follow me in the car. I told him it was hard to see around the bluffs in the dark, but he told me to get my butt in the truck and drive. I looked around and didn't see my mom anywhere. I drove to the bluffs and heard him honking. I looked in the rearview mirror and saw my dad waving and telling me to pull over. I put the truck in park and got out. Dad opened the trunk to the car and my mom got out. Next, he reached into the trunk and pulled out my wooden baseball bat and sat it on the ground. I got real scared about then. He dragged my mom over by me and told me to hang on to her. She was crying then. First time I ever remember seeing her cry. Then he got a paper sack out of the trunk and set it by the baseball bat. Next thing he did was put the car in neutral and pushed it off the bluff, down into the gully. By the time it landed it was all smashed up. He picked up the baseball bat and handed it to me. He told me that we needed to rid the world of such a worthless woman as my mom. He said that we deserved a better life. He said we needed a woman like Hannah Frye. I begged him to not make me do it, so he pulled a gun out of his pocket and told me that he could leave two dead people here or one. It was my choice. I closed my eyes, so I couldn't see her face, and hit her on her forehead as hard as I could. It broke the bat. He picked up the paper sack and then made me help him carry her body to the bottom of the gully where we put her in the car and made sure it looked like her head hit the windshield. He pulled pieces of her hair out of her head and smashed them into the broken glass. He walked out about two hundred yards and threw the baseball bat behind some rocks, put the sack on the ground by the car and opened the car door. He pulled a six pack of beer out of the sack and got one of the cans out of the box. Can we stop recording for a minute? Ok. Is it back on? Can I please have something to drink? Water is fine, thanks. So, is the recorder back on? Ok, where was I? The beer can. Yes, that's right. After he got the beer can opened he crawled in the car with my mom's body. He stuck his fingers in her mouth to pry it open and poured beer in it. He then opened the other cans, drank some beer from each of them, then poured the rest of it everywhere in the car. Then he threw the cans all over the place. When we got home he told me that I was now a murderer. He said that if my friends ever found out what I did they would go to the police and I would go to the electric chair. He said that Mookie Frye and Stoney Allen thought they were better than me and that I better not be friends with them because they would be the first ones to turn me in. He said if he ever saw me being nice to Mookie and Stoney again that he would turn me in to the police himself. Okay, so that's the story about my mom. Do I stop, or do you want me to keep talking? Keep talking? Okay, I guess now I will tell about the night my dad and I killed Stick Frye. Dad told me I couldn't ever go with him to the Frye's house, so I just stayed home by myself a lot. All he could talk about was Hannah. He said that he wanted to marry Hannah. I told him she was already married, and he said not for long. I didn't know what he meant by that. One evening after a baseball game he told me to get in the truck. He handed me a piece of rope that was rolled up. It was just about sundown when we drove over to the spot in the woods. He got out his binoculars and saw that Hannah's and Mookie's trucks were at their house. He looked down in their field and saw Stick in his tractor. Next, we drove through the gate that joined our property to the Frye's. Stick Frye's old tractor was stopped in the field and Stick had his head under the hood trying to fix something, so it would start up again. He was always working on that old tractor. Before we got out, my dad told me that I was already a murderer and he could have me sent to jail for the rest of my life. He told me we had to kill Stick Frye. He told me we needed to get him out of the way, so we could have a better life. He said that he was going to be talking to Stick and I was going to go around behind Stick and put the rope around his neck and strangle him. So that's what happened. I strangled him until he went limp. He wasn't able to put up much of a fight, with his bad leg and arm. He went pretty fast. I threw the rope down in the field. Dad and I moved Stick's body over to the side of the tractor that had the missing door. Then next we hooked a chain up to the tractor and pulled it over on him with the truck. The cab section fell right on him. Messed his body up pretty bad. We did that to make it look like an accident. Dad told me that he went back over after the coroner left and scattered a bunch of empty beer cans around, so it would look like Stick got drunk and rolled the tractor. I want to stop recording. I need to go to the bathroom. Is it back on? Okay, so do you want me to say my name and stuff again? Just start talking again? Okay. So, after the car bash I saw Frosty kissing Mookie and it made me really mad. I went home and went in the house and slammed the door hard. My dad came busting out of his bedroom asking me what the hell was going on. I told him about Frosty and he told me what he had just done to Hannah. He said we needed to take care of them both, once and for all. I was so mad at Mookie I didn't care if he lived or died. We got in the truck and drove over to our spot in the woods. My dad got out his binoculars and said he saw Hannah driving away. She was driving real slow so we waited until we made sure she was gone and drove over to her house. Dad knew where she hid a key, so he had me stay in the truck and keep watch while he went inside the house. He came out and left her front door wide open. I pointed that out to him and he told me to shut the hell up. When he got in the truck he handed me a pair of Mookie's cowboy boots and a package of Big League Chew. We waited until about ten o'clock that night and parked the truck over behind the filling station and walked over to the Liquor Store. I had the cowboy boots in my hands and stuck the Big League Chew in my back pocket and dad had a can of gasoline. He had me take my shoes and socks off and put the boots on and walk over behind the Liquor Store and find a big mud puddle. He came over to me and pushed on my shoulders, so I would sink down as far as I could. I steadied myself by holding on to him while I slipped off the boots. He told me to leave the boots in the mud and then he pulled the package of Big League Chew from my back pocket and threw it on the ground. Dad then walked over to the building, broke a window and climbed into the Liquor Store with the gas can. I stood watch while he was in there pouring the gasoline everywhere. He crawled out the window and threw the empty gas can back in the store. He looked over at me and started laughing. When he struck the match on his pants zipper, he smiled and whispered, "Thar she blows," and tossed the match through the window. It caught fire immediately. We stuck around a couple of minutes to make sure the fire was going good, then he told me to walk slow toward the truck. He said he didn't want anyone to see us running. After that, we drove to a pay phone and he made me call the police. I remember looking at my watch and saw that it was ten thirty. I told them the Liquor Store was on fire and hung up. That's it. That's my confession. I'll probably rot in jail the rest of my life. I guess that's what I deserve. I hope my dad gets the electric chair. He needs to fry. No, I don't want a Kleenex. Can we turn this thing off now?''

Butch Baxter was out in the field all day and did not see the sheriff's deputy cart Butch Ed away earlier in the day. Therefore, he was blindsided when he came up to the house around dark and saw a sheriff's deputy waiting for him on his front porch. He was handcuffed, read his rights, and not so carefully placed in the deputy's vehicle.

Stoney had also given the sheriff the investigation box they had stored away from Colleen Baxter's accident.

All the beer cans from Stick's accident and Colleen's accident, the baseball bat, and the rope were sent to the laboratory for DNA testing. The beer cans tested positive for Butch Baxter's saliva. The baseball bat tested positive for Butch Ed's DNA, and Colleen Baxter's blood and hair. The rope had Stick's DNA all over it.

Butch Baxter was given the death penalty. It would be by lethal injection, and not the electric chair, but his son, Butch Ed, was glad to hear that his dad was going to die either way.

The court was somewhat lenient with Butch Ed. He had fully cooperated with the authorities, and the death of his mother was when he was a minor, therefore he was sentenced to twenty years in prison, with the possibility of parole after fifteen.

CHAPTER 78:

The Blue Foam Finger

Deputy Pee Wee Ferguson had rearranged his schedule, so he could have the honor of putting the key in the jail cell to release Mookie Frye. The entire gang was present for the momentous occasion. Hannah, Stoney and Frosty Allen and their parents, Dan Wiseman, The Piper Landers Chapter of Students Against Drunk Driving, the Loopers brought grandma Marlene, Marilyn Maple and her family drove in from Miami, Mookie's entire senior class, Edwinna, Charley and Annie Bowman, and a whole passel of folks from Blackjack Hollow, stood on the courthouse steps to clap and cheer for the justice that had been brought to Mookie Frye.

A long caravan of cars followed Hannah's truck as she led the way back to Blackjack Hollow for the festive celebration. Dan Wiseman had arranged for a catered meal for everyone back at the Frye's farm. Hannah borrowed tables and chairs from their little Methodist church, and The Piper Landers Chapter of SADD helped her set it all up in the front yard.

They tied multi-colored balloons to all the chairs, and the tables were filled with food and cold Orange Crush.

Uncle Bud Looper prayed a beautiful prayer of thanksgiving for the blessings that had been bestowed on their beloved Mookie, and everyone sat down to enjoy the delicious feast.

Mookie had just chomped down on a crispy chicken leg when he noticed a black limousine pulling into their driveway. Rising out of the car from the sunroof was a huge blue foam finger emblazoned with KC Royals #1 Fan.

The windows of the car were tinted black, keeping the identities of the passengers a mystery.

Mookie Frye stood up as the car doors came open and out stepped none other than John Wathan and George Brett. Mookie thought he was surely going to faint.

The two men walked straight to Mookie and shook his hand.

George Brett handed Mookie the big blue foam finger. "Mookie Frye, we have brought you a royal blue foam finger that says KC Royals #1 Fan. We wanted to deliver this to you personally. You're probably thinking we are saying that you are the #1 fan of the Kansas City Royals."

Mookie interrupted with a robust, "I am!"

"Well, son, things aren't always as they seem. What we say this royal blue foam finger signifies is that the KC Royals are your #1 Fan! This organization started off watching your dad, Stick Frye, rock and fire every combination of pitches known to man, and some we were sure that he made up. He was a legend in his time, God rest his soul. And, now, Mookie, the minute the Kansas City Royals found out that Stick Frye had a son that was carrying on where his dad left off, we've been watching you too. We didn't want you to get away, so we are prepared to offer you a chance to come pitch for us. Are you interested?"

Everyone in the crowd answered for Mookie. It was a loud and proud, "Yes he is!"

George Brett and John Wathan joined in the food and festivities until almost dark. As they started to leave, Mookie asked if he could show them something. They were happy to oblige and followed Mookie to Stick's old barn.

They walked into the darkness as Mookie reached for the string to turn on the light. There on the wall was the poster of George Brett that had held a prominent place in Stick's barn for eighteen years.

"I'm thinkin' my dad would be real proud of me."

CHAPTER 79

They Forge a Bond

Annie Bowman poked her head out the back door and hollered at her husband, Charley, as he was trudging through the vegetable garden with an ancient walk behind cultivator. His hearing wasn't what it used to be, therefore Annie gave up after the third try and ventured closer, so he could hear.

"Charley, I just got off the phone with Mookie Frye. He's on his way over here to talk to you."

Charley told Annie he would finish the last row and head into the house when Mookie got there.

"Do you have any coconut cream pie left? That boy would probably love a slice."

Annie told Charley that she had just made a fresh one earlier in the morning, so Mookie would be set if he wanted some.

Mookie polished off two large pieces of Annie Bowman's delectable pie.

"Mrs. Bowman, that's probably the best pie I've ever had in my life. Thank you so much." Mookie laid his fork down on the china plate and rubbed his belly before he started his conversation with Charley and Annie.

"Charley, I had to come talk to you about some things that I'm puzzled about. I hope you can clear them up for me. I saw the box of stuff that Stoney brought to the sheriff. He told me you had given it to him. Where did you get those things? Especially the rope." Mookie hung his head for a moment at the mention of the rope that was used to strangle his father to death. "Where did you get the rope?"

Charley stood up and walked over to his easy chair to pick up his corncob pipe that was nestled in the bowl on the side table. He placed the pipe in his mouth, struck a match on the side of his overalls bringing it up to his pipe, and puffed until he got a good glow to the tobacco.

"Son, there's only one other person on this earth that I would tell what I'm going to tell, and it is you."

Mookie sat wide-eyed, with his body covered in goosebumps, as Charley Bowman divulged every single detail about his interaction with Bigfoot.

"I knew it. I knew this had to do with Bigfoot. He brought the stuff to you. He was an eye witness to the crimes and he knew someone needed to know. He trusts you, Charley. Oh, wow. Oh, wow. This is just unbelievable." Mookie was spellbound, as he thought about the possibilities of maybe someday interacting with Bigfoot himself.

CHAPTER 80:

The Setting Son

A month later, Mookie Frye was walking to his truck to load one of his dad's saddles into the back seat. The next day he would be heading to Kansas City, Missouri, to start training with the Kansas City Royals. An old friend of his parents had a small ranch outside of the city and they offered to let Mookie stay in one of their cabins while he was in town. They had plenty of horses for him to ride so he wanted to make sure he had one of his dad's saddles with him. Riding on one of his dad's saddles helped him feel a sense of peace. As he walked, he looked down at his BF cowboy boots. They were all shined up and beautiful. Boots Frye and Stick Frye, two of the best dads ever.

The sun was going down on the small farm in Blackjack Hollow, Oklahoma, as Mookie stopped in his tracks to survey the fields his father had lovingly managed for almost twenty years. Holding Stick's saddle with one hand and perching the other hand on his hip, Mookie Frye watched as the setting sun cast a faint glow on the entire vista. Stick was always excited with the change of seasons on his farm. Plowing, sowing seeds, reaping the bounty, and caring for the healthy herd of Black Angus cattle grazing over on the meadow, gave Mookie's dad a tremendous sense of accomplishment. Mookie remembered one of his dad's favorite sayings. "If you do what you love, you'll never work a day in your life."

As the shade of night settled in on the horizon, Mookie started thinking about how the sun goes down to signal the end of the day. Acknowledging to himself that the daylight never fails to wane, and every day always comes to an end. Over and over, and each day concludes with a different story. Some days overflow with joy, and some bring nothing but sorrow. Standing there in the moonlight, he gripped his dad's saddle and felt his father's spirit all around him. Mookie Frye vowed to go forward in his life with the desire to capture the same motivating force which propelled his dad and his granddad to leave such stellar legacies. He promised himself that he would never cease to grab each moment by the horns, to live life to the fullest, to spread joy wherever he would roam, and to welcome each new day with unbridled hope.

He felt hopeful. At that moment in time, Mookie knew he had a good grasp on the feelings that were washing over him. His heart ached for the things which happened that were out of his control, the things that he could not go back and change. Heartache coupled with hope. He was so humbled by the opportunities which had been given to him that were helping him realize his dreams. His future that had been secured by the unceasing persistence of his devoted father. His father who stopped at nothing to see to it that his son, Mookie, got his chance.

The contrast hit him and hit him hard. He leaned back against the fence and propped one foot behind him on the railing. He was suddenly overcome with profound sadness. So profound it almost took his breath away. With his eyes fixated on the starry sky, Mookie Frye's thoughts turned to Butch Ed Baxter. The young child which had innocently been catapulted into his father's evil scheme. Butch Ed had been powerless in trying to protect his mentally ill mother. He was helpless against his controlling and depraved father. Mookie Frye shuddered at the thought of what all Butch Ed and his mom had likely endured beyond the wooden screen door leading into the Baxter's house. Butch Ed had been ill equipped to handle the hand that he had been dealt. Mookie had been blessed. Butch Ed had been cursed…

Mookie was picturing himself in a Kansas City Royals uniform as he opened the door to his truck to load the saddle. The dome light in his pickup clicked on, casting a faint glow on the suitcases and boxes he had previously placed on the back seat. Tenderly positioning the leather saddle atop the nearest box, satisfied that his possessions were all tucked in and ready for tomorrow's drive, Mookie closed the truck door and turned to head back into the house.

He couldn't believe his eyes. Standing about ten yards from his truck, facing him in the glimmer of moonlight, he saw him. He was pointing at Mookie and then patting his own head. Mookie took off the Kansas City Royals baseball cap he was wearing and tossed it toward the hairy creature.

Bigfoot placed it on his head and trotted off into the night.

Other Titles by Martha Jordan Craig

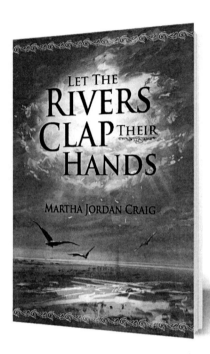

Available Nationwide in Paperback,
E-book and Audiobook

LET THE RIVERS CLAP THEIR HANDS

BY MARTHA JORDAN CRAIG

Let The Rivers Clap Their Hands is a masterfully woven saga of the emerging tale of two families from two very different backgrounds, each finding themselves freshly transplanted in the midst of Indian Territory in Oklahoma.

From the hardships of their pasts, to the wake of the Great Depression, to the dawn of World War II, these families' trials tell the tale of love, heartache, and hope.

Now you can take Mookie with you wherever you go...

THE SETTING SON

BY MARTHA JORDAN CRAIG

NOW AVAILABLE ON

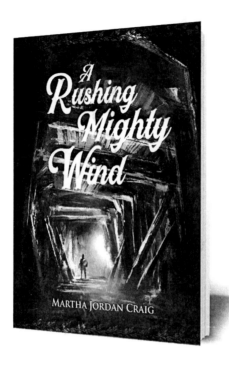

A RUSHING MIGHTY WIND

BY MARTHA JORDAN CRAIG

PROLOGUE

Mookie Frye, pitcher for the Colorado Rockies baseball team, had been Geocaching...

It all happened so fast. One moment he was standing at the opening to a cave, high in the Rocky Mountains of Colorado, and the next thing he knew, he was being attacked from behind. Stealthy assailants. They were like a band of Ninja warriors, swiftly knocking him forward into a face-plant, tying his hands behind his back, and jamming a cloth sack over his head. The sack had an acrid odor. Old and musty. Not a word was spoken.

One of his silent capturers pulled upward on his shirt collar signalling him to stand up, then prompted by a nudge to his back, he started to walk forward through an entrance to the underground chamber.

Blindly stumbling along, he had almost turned his ankle several times as his captors guided him deeper into the cave. He had no idea who was prodding him forward, but he was certain that the hard object being shoved into his back was a gun.

"Sit down." The voice was faint, but the tone, resolute.

He was led over to some type of boulder. It seemed to be about the same height as a chair by the way it felt behind his legs. Someone pushed his shoulders downward, signifying that he was to sit down. He complied, and the cloth sack was removed from his head. As his own vision adjusted, he could see a girl. A girl?

He was amazed at the steadiness in her hands as she pressed the barrel of the snub-nosed revolver firmly against his forehead. Mookie Frye looked her right in the eyes. Even in the shadowy darkness of the cave, he could see the black and shiny pupils of her eyes. Her eyes seemed to resemble the vacuous openings of a bottomless pit.

A swath of bangs hung listlessly to the side of her dirt-smudged face. She didn't flinch a bit and there was not one ounce of doubt in his mind that she would pull the trigger and blow his brains to smithereens if she felt the need. She couldn't be much more than twelve years old.

A voice in the darkness pierced the silence. This time, it was a woman's voice. "We knew you would come, Mookie Frye."